MW00808505

ZOMBIEGIRL ΩMEGA

INITIATION

ZOMBIE GIRL OMEGA – INITIATION

BOOK ONE OF THE ZETA WARS

O. T. Riesen

MARA PUBLISHING

The characters and events portrayed in this book are fictitious. Any similarity to real persons, living or dead, is coincidental and not intended by the author.

Copyright © 2023 Mara Publishing
All rights reserved

No part of this book may be reproduced, or stored in a retrieval system, or transmitted in any form or by any means, electronic, mechanical, photocopying, recording, or otherwise, without express written permission of the publisher.

Published by Mara Publishing
www.marapublishing,com

ISBN-13: 979-8-9872034-1-5

Library of Congress Control Number: 2023903299

Cover design by: O. T. Riesen

Printed in the United States of America

☾

For D & K.
My best creations.

✳

"Whoever said the pen is mightier than the sword obviously never encountered automatic weapons."

— DOUGLAS MACARTHUR

PROLOGUE

You could pinpoint, without doubt or confusion, exactly when the downfall of humanity occurred. It was a Thursday, innocuous and dull, save for a flash announcement broadcast across all forms of media. Something that changed the world's future and mine as well.

What follows is the personal account of myself and a handful of others—survivors like me.

ZOMBIE GIRL OMEGA – INITIATION

ACT 1
KEEP ON SURVIVING

OVERLOOK

A seamless wave of crystal blue ripples softly across the edge of a never-ending horizon of gold. Most people would have said the sight was beautiful. Breath-taking, even. A striking example of nature's majesty and wonder. Those people are dead now, and frankly, I hate sand. For that matter, I'm not a fan of people, either.

With a raspy sigh, I scratch half-heartedly at the muck-brown flak vest encasing my upper torso. Perpetual chafing is one of the many joys experienced here, at the end of the world—that and dehydration. Attempting to lick chapped lips, my tongue practically glues itself to the inside of my mouth.

After all this time, you'd think I'd be used to having a throat comprised mostly of sandpaper, with no respite in sight. No such luck. I still have that gut-deep longing for a chilled glass of straight-out-of-the-tap, ultra-purified water, no matter how long I've been out here.

Alas, the only barrier I have for keeping my body from imitating a raisin in this unforgiving heat is the re-filtered stuff that we are outfitted with by Regs. Composed of filtered moisture from the suit and the condensation that night brings to the desert, the resulting water ration is something that one both equally thirsts for and dreads. Water is the key to staying alive out here; unsurprisingly, it's rarely found in this wasteland.

The manufactured liquid meets the function. However, it greatly leaves something to be desired taste-wise. The now-defunct FDA would probably insist upon a warning label or, at the minimum, including bodily refuse as the main ingredient. I've heard it called 'borderline piss' by other Zeta soldiers, but I'm not picky enough to care. Living takes priority over semantics.

I, for one, am begrudgingly thankful to have whatever is available, regardless of how it's achieved. You learn to set your expectations low in the military as it makes day-to-day life more exciting and fulfilling in the long run. I missed my calling as a marketing specialist. That one would have been perfect for some GD recruitment poster. Maybe in my next life.

The well-worn leather hide of my mesh glove scratches roughly against my forehead as I wipe my hand across a sweat-soaked brow. The material absorbs some of the perspiration by chance, leaving the rest to be moved uselessly along the hairline. Eyes fixed once more upon the wavering image of the town that awaits me further down this dust-entombed road, I replace my equally dusty helm, snapping it firmly into place and concealing myself from the world at large.

It's always the same routine—the slick slide of metal on metal accompanied by a soft click; a press to the left and then again to the right produces two more clicks. The crinkle of leather follows as the lab-cooked animal hide is pulled taut around a clasp covering the gap left between helm and shoulder. One more tap to the outside of the helm, and I hear the familiar, three-toned chime as the HUD activates, bringing the world around me into sharp focus.

By habit, I lower the pitch of my audio to reduce the scratch and skip of a silent Comms line. It will be a good half hour before I'm back in reliable communication range with my teammates. Assuming there are no unplanned interruptions, the four of them will be in position around the same time I am.

Glancing to the right, I take in the matte mocha beast that is my All-Terrain Cycle, or ATC to be cute with acronyms. Its patiently waiting form is a reliable comfort, even if half the time I look like some small child straddling it. One size does not fit all.

With one more vertebrae-popping stretch, break time's over. I climb onto the massive back of my bike, engaging its hybrid engine. The low hum that greets me is a welcome return to what passes for civilization and helps to set my head into a suitable space. I miss the loud, grand rumble of a gas-powered Harley, but times change, and the past can no longer hold an electric fuse to the present.

ARRIVAL

The last several miles of my approach to destination ghost town whatever (Zee town number 325, my SITREP informs) gives me time to recenter both myself and my thoughts. It's essential to be in the right mindset when entering enemy territory, no matter who the opposition is. Going alone for this first part of the mission leaves me in an uncomfortable position with the locals, number-wise.

You would think with severely crippled higher-brain function, my enemy would pose less of a threat. After all, I have the advanced weaponry and the know-how for putting it to good effect. However, there are a lot more of them than there are of me. I can't tell you how many, as that number constantly changes. Hence why Zeta soldiers don't rely on numbers alone—we divide and conquer.

The thrum of the hybrid's chassis can barely be heard over the whoosh of air passing by my helm. Its vibrations travel up my thighs in ripples, the throttle practically matching my pulse. My torso lightly tingles where flesh meets material, but thankfully the two-piece bodysuit is practically grafted to my body. The protective material, essential to every Zeta soldier uniform, is a kind of synthetic 'silk' designed to act like a spider's webbing, only multi-layered and much more robust. Nothing like the chain mail garb of the Dark Ages.

In reality, there is no way to entirely protect soft and vulnerable human skin against the constant rub of any material. I also do not recommend being continuously enveloped in thick leather in the middle of high desert at all hours of the day. Tell me that you won't sweat like a pig set deep in a Polynesian barbecue pit. I dare you. Then again, spend a day without proper protection in this environment, and you'll resemble beef jerky the next sunrise.

My destination is now all that remains in my HUD's sight.

It's unchanged from a few days ago when we initially observed it from afar. The glaring light of a cloudless sky, coupled with an unforgiving sun, does little to obscure my vision. Optical lenses are explicitly tuned to optimize my viewing experience, taking care of any blind spots or lens flares. The sensors that line my helm's outer surface register the air's temperature, humidity, and wind speed. What I wouldn't give to feel it pushing against my face and streaming through my hair. Forget the useless stats.

Finally, the derelict edge of town nears, and I let the gentle whine of my ATC die, coasting to a stop by a sign that is faded to a shade of yellow resembling mustard. The grayed-out writing is almost illegible. Tilting my head, I attempt to decipher the small snippets. Something about Nevada being the "Friendliest" and "Loneliest."

Well, that's just sad. Those words probably announced something grander about this place at some point. From where I sit, it looks like the set of an old Western, complete with big all-caps letters and white railings. Other than what must have been a courthouse at some point, most buildings top off at a couple of stories. Honestly, I don't even bother to store my observations—there's no point. Not a speck of life flourishes here and probably won't for some time. I think even the flies have given up.

My gloved hand runs along the right side of my cycle to where it meets an indentation somewhat bigger than my thumb. Lightly depressing an unmarked button, a compartment swings out to the side, revealing a stash of slightly worse-for-wear audio players. You know, those old, fashionably tiny kinds. The first one my questing fingers latch onto, I snag, resealing the storage compartment so that it's once again a flush and seamless part of my bike. After a quick check to ensure there's still enough juice left in the battery for a last hurrah, I secure the device to the back of that forgotten sign with a bit of adhesive putty.

Throwing one last look around—nothing wrong with being cautious—I crank the volume knob to its highest setting and hit the "play" button. Classic Rage Against the Machine blasts loudly from the stereo's small but effective speakers. It's amazing how much noise one of these things can produce. Not GOOD noise, of course. Data files have nothing on audio crystals, in my humble opinion.

Ah well. No time to be a snooty audiophile.

Kicking my bike into life, I swing its front around in a sharp "U" before tearing down the dusty road and back from whence I came. Tattered buildings blur by reflecting a healthy mix of the different decades they originated from. The taller, more modular office buildings lurk every so many blocks, providing some integrated interruption. I snort at the thought. None of these structures are 'tall' by city standards—six stories classifies as a skyscraper, locally. Turning the accelerator up another gear, the muted grays and washed-out reds blur by as I pass the few remaining buildings that face the main drag. They're quickly left behind, along with a cloud of brown froth the front tank treads of my ATC kick up in their wake.

Both sensors and eyes continuously scan shattered, street-level windows and dark alleyways for movement. But no, the cracked and weed-strewn sidewalks are bare of anything that could pass for a threat.

Once I've determined that I'm far enough out, I open my bike up fully and break off from my initial path to cut a wide arc around the town. This move lands me near the opposite end of where I was, but that's intentional. The entire trip doesn't take more than ten minutes—enough time to allow for adrenaline to pump resolutely through my system.

An overturned semi beckons to me from its final resting place. It's the perfect spot to set up and wait. Once again, I kill my bike, silently gliding to a stop behind it. Quickly, I dismount from the beast's metal back to tuck my form into the shelter the Peterbilt's horrendous blue and red wreckage provides. Now, it's time to wait.

Time passes unbroken by either sound or movement. It could be minutes or a half-hour. A vague noise begins to register in my audios. It gains in volume before turning into a noticeable racket of groaning and shuffling. There isn't much longer to wait. I press my form closer to the ground—part training, part instinct.

Then, like a light switching on inside my head, I know they're here.

Every sense that I call my own detects their approach, from the vibrations of the ground to the taste of mildew riding the slight breeze. They filter down the town's main street, seemingly disorganized in their mass march, but there always seems to be a single-mindedness to their actions. It is as if there's a pathway clear to them that they all somehow know to follow unquestioningly.

Most drag themselves slowly, their emaciated body weight still far too heavy for starved muscles to carry. Each one's dull eyes are red and vacant of any semblance of sentience. Heads misshapen by random protrusions and divots, facial features as skewed as an impressionist's subject matter might be. Their groaning is the guttural sound that results from air being pushed through a half-open maw by the effort of moving—of artificially extended non-existence.

The listless parade goes toward my little noise maker for a good twenty minutes before the crowd begins to thin down and peter off. A businessman and what looks to be a female doctor—stethoscope and all—make up the rear of the procession. They're probably lagging at the back of the pack because mister suit-and-tie is missing his left foot from the joint of the ankle down, and the doc seems burdened by a deep laceration across her middle. The bloat of her internals pressing against the open black wound is pretty disgusting, but the part of my mind that protests at the sight has learned to shut the hell up over time.

Obvious physical impairments are noted as points of weakness. Not that it'll make much of a difference momentarily.

I carefully get into position, drawing one of my two side arms from its holster along my right thigh. The well-oiled leather is wonderful— stiff and worn, it hardly rustles and offers little resistance along my gun's barrel. My left-hand clasps and steadies its counterpart as I line up the first target.

Breathe in.

Breathe out.

Fire.

Thunk

The near-simultaneous thud of a bullet first entering, then exiting, bone greets me as my shot drills a neat hole through the first one's skull. Another inaudible 'pop' and the doctor joins the cooling body in the three-piece suit on the dusty ground, limbs akimbo.

I know my shots are well and true, so I don't bother firing a second or third round. Ammunition is too precious to waste on paranoia. Instead, I'd rather hunt the rest of these monsters down the old-fashioned way.

The rhythmic pounding of my feet hitting the covered pavement echoes hollowly as I sprint along row upon row of empty downtown shops. The once-black ground is riddled with large cracks running deeply everywhere from the near-constant dry heat and lack of regular TLC. Isn't it strange how the streets of ancient Rome somehow managed to outlast these modern asphalt ones, so slick and high-tech in comparison?

The next block's worth of buildings provides a nice, clear line-of-sight to the end goal. I press myself into its shadow to hide from the townsfolk and the midday sun, keeping an eye on the skyline. Two more of my kind should be parked on top of the buildings keeping track of this progression: my demo lady, Chi, and our gunner and perpetual pain in my ass, Rho. Breathing even and measured to my ears, I follow the trail of the undead, carefully weaving between structures at a controlled and deliberate pace.

The group is noticeably slowing in their disjointed trek, as a quick peek around the next corner confirms my suspicions. I catch sight of what looks like a slight pile-up forming. Their blank faces reflect none of the confusion that their herd is experiencing. They simply meander about aimlessly at the intersection just ahead, waiting for a sign as to where to go next.

I take in the lack of activity on the street. After a quick scan from one side of the road to the other, I push myself to the lee of the building opposite me. An overhang provides relative safety, and I use the opportunity to grab a breather before the real chaos begins.

BOOM

Rifle kept snugly over my right shoulder, I feel along the painted brick wall behind me and find an indentation my gloved fingers can wedge into. Reaching up and not cursing my lack of height for the first time, I climb up the side using whatever nook or cranny presents itself. There is no fatigue or burn from my muscles at the quick ascent as I reach the rooftop. I could still be standing in the same place below for all my body knows or cares.

From this new position, I make out the horde of brain dead townsfolk milling aimlessly around the itty-bitty stereo, clueless of the how or why. Such obliviousness on the part of everyday people would have been far from uncommon in a past life. It's funny, considering these   were ordinary people, and as Zee, they're equally out of touch with the present. A tragic reminder of the mess that humans have become.

A glint catches my left eye. My second's sand-colored helmet is visible from his selected spot on a dark, flat roof four or five buildings down from me. Rho notices my observation of him and throws a hearty wave before miming shooting me with his gloved right hand.

Joy. At least he has the sense not to point a loaded weapon at his Commanding Officer. Small miracle. More than likely, he's just avoiding the lecture that will await him after the mission. I have a talent for browbeating that I take great pride in.

Purely out of habit, a sigh escapes me as I shake my head at his antics. Settling onto one knee, I ready myself. The stock of my rifle is solid and sure as I pull it down and draw it into my shoulder, peering through the scope. A quick scan of our surroundings and everything seems ready for the next stage. I can't see the team's demolition specialist, but I sure as hell feel confident issuing the command to her.

"Chi, we're green."

Even though I speak softly into my helm's microphone, my voice projects perfectly across the airwaves to the Comms channel the others are signed onto.

There is a short click and then, "Roger that. Commencing. Fire in the hole."

Within seconds, the ground erupts in ripples, and the outskirts of the town becomes a ring of flame and carnage. For that brief instant, the sound is deafening and all-consuming.

A large plume of black smoke rises steadily and unyielding in its climb. The blast's aftermath is a symphony of complete, blessed silence. But it is not over yet. Waiting for the dark cloud to disperse in the light breeze while the debris settles, I focus on ground zero through my rifle's sight and look for those familiar stumbling silhouettes.

I have no doubt I'll find them. Perhaps not surprisingly, there are always survivors (I use the term loosely here). Their numbers vary between the few and the not-so-few, with no decipherable pattern for which outcome to expect. It's always a roll of the dice where they gathered in proximity to the ordinance. The question is simply how many? The absolute stillness of this moment can be nerve-wracking, but I let it soak into the very center of my being. All that I hear is the tempo of my breathing—deep and even. My heart beats in sync at a steady adagio.

Panic and anxiety are a couple of the first emotions that the UF (the United Forces to civvies) vigorously works to train out of their soldiers in Basic. If you can't comply, you're too much of a liability to keep around in this line of work. Enhanced soldiers are easily worth a couple dozen of the standard kind—hell, probably even more than that.

Why would the UF waste time, energy, and good food on someone who won't shut up and get in line? I never tested it myself to find out. I have no compunctions calling myself a UF pawn, as that is what we all are.

The air has thinned out enough to distinguish a couple of nondescript forms mulling about the blackened perimeter. Straightening up, I wait until a disfigured head missing its left ear enters my crosshairs. Just like that, I shoot Van Gogh, and it becomes a Jackson Pollock. I line up the following form just as succinctly and take it out.

Another townsperson's head snaps back and hair and bits of flesh fly as they slump motionlessly to the ground. Following the bullet's path, I can tell that Rho is taking care of things adequately from his end, doing more or less the same as I am. That's one less variable for me to worry about. He has a nasty habit of interpreting my orders creatively.

Our systematic attack runs like clockwork. We choose our targets, sight, then fire, carrying on in this vein for as many minutes as it takes to get the job done. Each shot is fatal. No bullet is wasted. Together, we create a beautiful, rhythmic cacophony deeply ingrained within each of us. Without breaks, we never miss a beat.

Another thing that the UF beats into you: there's no room for mistakes. To err means to forfeit your life, or worse—your teammates' lives.

CLEAN UP

My chronometer tells me that no more than ten minutes have passed since the start of this skirmish. The earth still smolders from the earlier fire bath, courtesy of Chi. A noticeable pause to the noise that has been a constant ranged assault on my audios has me surveying the scene below.

Smoke lingers thick and dark, covering the ground and our handiwork, but as it's gently blown away, I can finally get a clear view of the land below. From my vantage point, all the Zee appear to have been dealt with. Gobs of what can only be congealed blood mixed with the upturned dirt, creating a disgusting floor of muck and carnage, but nothing moves. That's all I care about at the moment.

"Clear," I breathe into my mic.

Rho's response is quick, "Clear."

"Clear." Chi echoes, following the gunner.

"Alright. Let's do one last sweep from north to south and pick off any stragglers. Chi, keep to the eastern edge of the city. Omicron and Mu, follow Rho and me. Let's keep the line tight, people."

My team sends their confirmations, one after another.

"Roger."

"Affirmative."

"Will do."

"Okay!" Mu's chipper voice at the end has me rolling my eyes—not that my teammates can appreciate the gesture, sadly. How anyone can be so happy in the middle of this purgatory is beyond me.

We proceed reasonably quickly through the town. Our movements are not overly hurried, but we're not precisely dawdling. My decoy did its job well, as we run into no resistance on our closing sweep. Even though we move away from the explosion's epicenter, the air is thick with the scent of singed hair, all things rotten, and charbroiled flesh. I can't say I've gotten used to that particular flavor. The stench has the power to undo a seasoned soldier, leaving them at odds with their environment. Imagine being stuck in a room full of dying people with no flushing toilet or shower in sight.

Yeah, it's like that.

Catching movement out of the corner of my right eye—peripheral always gets more of a reaction in the brain than straight-on line-of-sight—I swing my rifle barrel smoothly to the side 90 degrees and finger the trigger.

A creature slides slowly along some ma and pa store's wall to keep its decomposing corpse propped up. The thing makes its sluggish way toward me, leaving little bits and pieces of itself on the broken siding of the building. Not bothering with the rifle slung over my shoulder, I draw one of my two sidearms, take careful aim, and fire. Its head jerks with the impact, a spray of thick red coating the wall behind it before the mass of rags and filth crumples to the ground— positively dead this time.

The mistake that many make, both amateur and seasoned professionals, is to allow themselves to become captivated by the Zee. Their behavior—like our own yet primitive and unexpected in its animalistic nature—has a habit of enrapturing the unchanged. So much so that they dismiss the danger they're in.

I don't think that anyone has quite figured out if they're capable of intentional communication with each other, let alone setting a trap. Sociologists, those who are still called by that moniker, have their work cut out trying to analyze these creatures to determine if there is anything left of the higher being that they once were. My gut shouts out a solid "NO." Having experienced the disgusting pleasure of sharing personal space with the Zee, I can decisively state that they've never shown even the barest hint of humanity. Just a set of mindless, gnashing jaws on legs.

Stray gravel crunches loudly under the heel of my boot as I turn and move past the laid-out body. Once again, my handgun is appropriately stowed in the holster along my thigh, rifle back in hand in a ready position. With my senses extended to the best of my ability, I take in the environment around me, being open to any shifts or changes in sound. In the more functional sense, being a good listener is an essential skill to have in your arsenal. It ranks up there with opposable thumbs. Not because many in this day and age need some shoulder to cry on. I dare anyone to try that shit with me.

Intently, I listen for anything out of the ordinary. Wind blocked by a body or the telltale scrape of a well-seasoned Zee trying to move its rotting carcass toward its next meal. My team maintains radio silence as they, too, canvass the site. Mu should be picking off the shambling stragglers from the rise above this town via her sniper rifle. Omicron will be standing next to her—an imposing presence, acting as both backup and an extra set of eyes to guard her six. His secondary task is to scout for any remaining Zee via his helm's sights and relay their positions to the three of us living who walk among the dead.

Rho and Chi should be doing the same as I am on the opposite border of this town, closing off the escape route to any of our prey that feels like going for a stroll elsewhere. I pulled the short straw this time, so I have the center stretch to cover. This part of the mission is always the tensest for me as we move from structure to structure, seeking the leftovers to dispose of. It's the perfect time for a Zeta soldier to be ambushed and picked off. It's as if Zee can recall just how vulnerable humans are when they're solo.

Most of the time, that's one thing I don't have to worry about with my team. We keep our guard up, especially when separated in enemy territory. One misjudgment can send the whole megillah sideways, resulting in a lost teammate—a brother. So long as it's within my control, I refuse to leave any of mine unprotected and out of reach.

We are Zeta soldiers—all of the Zee's strengths and none of their weaknesses. In particular, that nasty tendency towards cannibalism and a certain lack of higher brain function. In the UF, you don't make it out of the gates from Conversion if you take too well to the upgrade.

There were twenty-five other soldiers in my Conversion batch. I didn't know any of them before the procedure (no birth names or faces). That whole time was a blur in my history. Of our batch, only five became Zeta soldiers and were assigned to a squad. I was the twenty-second dosed, converted, and enhanced—Omega22. The Omega symbol is a permanent brand on my neck.

The telltale pops of guns being discharged from elsewhere in this ghost town jolts me out of my reverie. I pay close attention to their cadence. They're single shots—even and measured in their timing. That informs me that the shooter is in control of the situation and unhurried in their actions. It means less for me to worry about, so I get to work clearing out the few Zees remaining. The last walking corpse in the vicinity falls by my hand, dust puffing up at the impact its body makes upon the ground.

To be safe, I run a tight thermal scan from my helm of the surrounding area, searching for any signs of life. It confirms what my heightened senses already know—the gentle townsfolk are no more. I embrace the utter silence that greets me. Breathe in, breathe out. The stillness is perfect.

I can finally feel some of the tension that has built in my muscles throughout the day release. Most of it's me internalizing and not intentional by any means. It's difficult to remember that my teammates are not the only ones I need to keep a pulse on—my body and mind also require monitoring.

I call for a status update and receive four positive pings in reply. Each chirp provides an added measure of relief. Gloved hand rising to my headset, I activate the Comms line and give my teammates the 'all clear.' Slinging the rifle back over my right shoulder, I meander back to where my bike is stashed.

Moisture beads on my throat as the sweat starts to collect along my nape. The walk doesn't take me nearly as long as the original trek did. I'm not avoiding dried leaves and twigs underfoot or searching broken windows for the reflection of something gruesome. That probably helps. The sun has reached its zenith, and I get to my ATC not a moment too soon.

Removing the always-present helm is a blessing in disguise. I let out a sigh of relief at the warm air tickling the shorter hairs plastered to the back of my neck. A flash of light from the overgrown weeds near my boots catches my interest and has me dropping to one knee, drab bronze helmet tucked into the crook of my left arm. Pushing the dirt around, I unearth a slender chain, coaxing it from its final resting spot. The shiny object resists for a moment before jerking free, a small medallion no bigger than a quarter hanging from its middle.

As the flat oval spins slightly on its chain, a dusty, inlaid photo is revealed on the flip side. A young girl stares back at me, nestled between the loving arms of her parents. Reassessing the chain it's on, it could probably only wrap around my wrist once. Not an adult's necklace.

Rising with the small bauble hanging limply from my grasp, I turn and come face to face with a snarling visage of discolored and wrinkled flesh. My hand drops to my sidearm, but I know I won't be fast enough. Its teeth sink into the stiff leather of my raised gauntlet before a trill cuts through the air, followed closely by the Zee's knee blowing out in a shower of bone fragments and tendon. The creature sways haphazardly to the side from the loss of physical support, and a second bullet drills a perfect hole through its forehead. Its body spasms in its last throes before finally lying in a motionless heap at my feet.

The sudden crackling of an open Comms line echoes from my helm's position on the ground. With a start, my hand twitches to its counterpart. Wincing at my inattentiveness, I retrieve the helmet and bring its audio close to my ear.

"Doing a little window shopping, Commander?"

I feel my mouth draw downwards as I scan the roof line of the surrounding area. It doesn't take long to pick out Rho's tall form several buildings down from my position, helm still covering his head.

"What the fuck are you doing up there, Rho? Get the hell on your bike now and move out!"

"That's not a nice way to say "thank you.""

"NOW, Rho!" I almost chip the edge of one of my front teeth.

"Whatever you say, boss!"

The low growl that rises from my throat is purely a subconscious reaction to fools and foolishness. In disgust, I toss the trinket back down to its former home and dismiss it from my thoughts just as quickly. The stupid thing damn nearly cost me my neck.

By straddling the beast in preparation for hauling out of here, my proximity unlocks the engine and kicks it into gear. As I pass the small crater that used to be the entrance to this town stuck in permanent limbo, I am joined by two other bikes.

Without looking, my sensors inform me that Rho is on my right and Chi to the left. As we draw by the ridge overlooking our mission, the last two riders complete the convoy—Mu in the middle and Omicron bringing up the rear. This is what we do. Not that there are many left to care.

BACK AT CAMP

The ride back to our camp is uneventful and blissfully quiet. Each team member is focused on their thoughts, and I let them be for now. There's no room for remorse when doing these kinds of missions. Our enemy is neither clever nor well-armed. It doesn't desire a peaceful coexistence with the leftovers of the human race. They are not us, and we are not them. The Zee are a plague to humanity, and if we don't rid our world of their kind, hope for a civilized future isn't realistic. I feel no remorse about their destruction—they're already gone.

When the sun is in its slow descent towards the horizon, we pull into a small circle of one-person tents nestled at the base of a rock formation. The slight rise is higher than any of the buildings in the town we just cleansed, so nestled as we are at its base, our presence is hidden here. As we dismount, there is much joking and elbowing between the soldiers. My team's overall mood lifted during our two-hour ride. After dismounting, I grab a square of microfiber cloth, no bigger than my palm, and give the bike's main panels a quick rub down. Best to keep it clear of dust for optimum solar absorption tomorrow.

The five metal monstrosities we rode in on are positioned along the edge of our encampment. Each ATC is equipped with motion detectors accurate to 30 feet and low-pitched personal alarms designed to draw our attention, not the Zee. These are our best and only warning systems for intruders.

Once my bike is clean and clear, I address the scout.

"Chi, get word to HQ that site B6EX25 has been successfully scrubbed and prepped."

"Will do, Commander." The lean femme gives me a twitch of her lips that might be a smile and a nod before heading to the radio equipment. She passes by Mu as the sniper jogs to my location, bright and shiny grin firmly in place.

"Great job, Omega!"

"Yeah, especially that last Zee, boss."

My expression morphs as I glare sourly at Rho's entrance into my personal space. Unrepentantly, he smirks back while the indigo-haired femme asks him what he means, oblivious to the background behind our conversation. Of course, given the opportunity and a quasi-captive audience, Rho will run with it as far as he can, and he proceeds to do just that. Mu sadly feeds Rho's malfunction by listening with rapt attention.

He expounds upon a wholly ludicrous and utterly deniable tale of the last Zee standing. The one that nearly ingested my brain had it not been for his selfless act of heroism that undoubtedly saved me from "Certain Death"—his words, not mine.

Knowing that the lanky gunner can and probably will continue regaling the team with this little story on into the night, I elect to nip it in the ass now. His monologue is cut off mid-word as he blinks stupidly at the pistol, whose business end is currently point-blank between his eyes.

"Omega!" Mu gasps, managing to impart through the sound of my name both supreme offense and shock in the same breath. Not like the guy didn't have it coming.

I hold my sergeant's gaze, daring him to continue in the same vein. His hands rise steadily into the space before him, palms forward in the universal sign of bitch ass surrender. With him back at a more tolerable level, I allow the gun to tilt forward so that its butt is presented to Rho.

Message received.

"Since you have nothing better to do, why don't you see to cleaning my gun and bike?" I do my best to keep my expression as flat as possible. Leaving him with said weapon, I turn and go a few strides before Rho finally registers what I said.

"Hey! That's not fair!" The whining quality of his voice doesn't phase me at this point in our time together.

Not bothering to face him, I throw one last retort over my shoulder. "I'm not fair, Rho. You should have figured that out by now."

Omicron gives me a high five as I pass him, having witnessed the short drama that preceded.

"You can clean my bike while you're at it, man," the big guy adds helpfully, clapping the slightly taller and much skinnier Rho hard on the shoulder.

As medic continues to tease gunner, I make my way to the tan pup tent that offers a bit of respite. The tents are little more than a propped-up body bag that protects us from insects and the elements while providing a slice of privacy for proper resting. Being the mobile unit we are, pretty much all our gear is lightweight, versatile, stows easily, and is kept to a minimum. We only get to pull these suckers out when we're stationary for more than a couple of days. Otherwise, it's all sleeping bags under the stars…vertically speaking, that is.

Once the 'door' is unzipped, I take a quick scan inside and find everything as I left it. I make as if to enter before habit kicks in, and I remember what must be done first and foremost. Rolling back onto my heels, I procure a black felt pen from one of my many vest pockets and draw a simple skull and bones on the side of my tent no bigger than a half dollar.

The doodle matches the many columns and rows of similar graphics I have added to personalize my space over the years. Each skull and bones is another town like today—a place cleared of death, waiting to be reborn one day.

ACT 2
WHAT'S LEFT BEHIND

A NEW MISSION

The team is restless. Of late, our missions have been an unmitigated waste of our collective time and skills. Not to mention that the marked increase in idle time is ill-advised when you're isolated in a barren land with a bunch of crazies. And no, I don't mean the Zee. They're downright sane compared to the team of soldiers that I command.

Rho has become increasingly creative in expressing his boredom. Consequently, he's irritating the hell out of everyone. Omicron found several of the spare hypodermic needles from supplies super glued to the front of his bike (plunger and all) like some sad-looking porcupine. It's not often that the big man is anything less than congenial, but after discovering his little 'present,' I was almost sure I would be down a man by the end of the day. Medic he may be, but that only makes the punishments he doles out more interesting.

And painful. Definitely painful. Don't piss off the man responsible for administering your allotted painkillers.

One of my gunner's more typical targets, Mu, found candy wrappers from her favorite and much coveted hard candy strewn about the inside of his tent, his sleeping bag, and of course, Rho himself. The idiot was passed out in the middle of it all, taking a cat nap when she went to wake him for duty. There must have been a couple of classes I slept through during high school biology because I had no idea that the human face could turn so many shades of red.

I still don't know what he did to Chi, but I would be avoiding sleep for the foreseeable future if I were him. She glared at his person unrelentingly in a way that promised a prolonged and painful death for him.

Eh. He probably deserves it.

It is easy to forget that although the dark-haired scout is typically low-key. She can be extremely devious and outright sinister, given the proper catalyst and focus. I suppose that I should intervene in some manner. It won't do for my team to drop down to four. I need as many living bodies as possible under my command, no matter how warped and masochistic they are.

Scanning the cramped interior space of my tent, I look for anything amiss, particularly among those possessions that I give a damn about. Rho likes to go for those. Why waste time with trivialities when you can stab them in the heart? The pointy-haired bastard has been stealing looks my way all morning, and when we make eye contact, he gets this shit-eating grin.

It's a face that I'd like to punch, as I've found precisely the stupidity he has inflicted upon me.

My pencils.

My hard-to-come-by, rarely-see-the-light-of-day pencils are firmly embedded into the toe of one of the standard, military-issue tan socks I own. A slightly off-kilter grumpy face with beady, angry eyes has been lovingly sketched into the padded part of each sock. The portion of my mind not fritzing distantly notes that the shafts of the pencils have been strategically placed at various angles to mimic how my hair loves to behave.

That little rat bastard has gone several leaps too far.

By this point, I am seething. After gracelessly reverse crawling out of my mummy tent, I march through the campsite to shred one Sergeant's ass. As if sensing the black aura and the impending death that is me, I catch movement out of the corner of my eye—Rho attempting to melt into the side of Mu's dust-gray tent. Fists clenched, I stomp my shit-brown, thick-soled boots to his location. He knows by now that it is better not to run from me.

This behavior may seem childish to the casual observer, but I've never cared about the opinions of others. My hands itch with the desire to wring his neck, and I've just got an excellent, firm grip on his poncho before the Comms unit shrieks to life. Mu, the closest to the equipment, neatly shifts the handset away from the antiquated piece of junk to stop the shrill cry of feedback. Well, that's unexpected.

Turning my attention back to Rho, I regard him as a specimen I would like to dissect. One dirty finger points at his face, promising retribution later. It takes some inner strength and soul-searching, but I manage to release my death grip on his person and make my way toward the Comms unit. Rho may feel that he's gotten off the hook, but I rarely, if ever, forget any transgressions, and he knows it. Breathing deeply to center myself, I casually flick the switch over to 'receive' and grab the small, handheld mic.

An authentication code comes through the garbled mess of static— barely decipherable, save to trained ears with enhanced hearing. Mu, our sniper, with her secondary role as a Comms person, pulls out a sad and tattered thing that vaguely resembles our encoded reference book, flipping quickly through its pages before stopping on one. Patiently, I wait as she scans the content, short finger tracing the trail that her eyes follow. Making a mini noise of triumph in her throat, she quickly looks up at me and nods sharply, flipping the book my way to share. I promptly memorize the authorization code printed in neat, slab letters.

"Base Camp One-Eight, this is Beta Squad 226, authorization Bravo Niner Two Hero."

Another burst of static garbles the line. By this time, the remaining two squad members have left their posts to listen in. I choose not to comment as we're currently in a relatively safe zone. The line clears noticeably, and then I hear the Colonel's crisp and authoritative voice over the transmission.

"Beta Squad 226, you are to perform an SR at coordinates Zulu Four-One, Charlie Six-Eight-Two. Alpha Team confirmed engagement with enemy Zee at oh-eight hundred hours, nine days ago, and missed their check-in with HQ. Expect a six-man Alpha unit and assume hostile Zee at the location." His nasally tone is so calm and detached. The guy could be delivering a weather report for all of the difference it would make to him. The result would probably be as accurately forecast.

An SR, huh? Search & Retrieval missions aren't conducted often in our line of work. It's not that Zeta soldiers like us are undervalued. Far from it. We represent a significant investment of time and resources by the United Forces, neither of which they prefer to waste. This focus explains why I spent nearly a year training to be what I am today before being released into the world. Let me explain. Once a team is critically compromised, whether on a mission or not, it's usually not worth the effort and risk to retrieve them. There's not much left to recover. For this team to have been out of contact for over a week, let's say that things are looking grim for them.

Whoever they are. This team holds enough standing with the 'Powers That Be' to rate a personal rescue. Nine days, though? Even the best of us would have difficulty surviving a week alone in an overrun Zee sector, and boy is Zulu-Charlie nothing less than the seventh circle of hell.

The boys in stats estimate that not a single person managed to make it out of city limits unchanged—not one. Not a man, woman, child, senior citizen...well, you catch my drift. That spread of the Zee mutation is precisely what you'd expect to happen in a heavily populated area, like all the big cities and tourist traps. Regardless of my squishy feelings, I know that command has been hard up on taking that sector back for quite some time. I hadn't realized how desperate they were to do so— my mistake.

With the limited intel of that zone, this could be a suicide run for my team—something I'm not on board with. If we take an obscene risk, I'd prefer it to be on our terms.

"Base Camp One-Eight, please advise on the size and positions of known Zee cells, over," I immediately respond. No sense wasting time chit-chatting as this Colonel is never one for base gossip. That's fine by me. Just give me what I need to succeed.

Omicron, Chi, and Rho crowd in and join Mu and me at the Comms unit. We all are eager to know what we're up against. But the longer we wait with no honest info, the more I lose faith that we'll be handed the data we depend upon to do our job well. Such knowledge is vital to successfully navigating enemy territory. Going in blindly on "hope" is not a plan.

A minute goes by, then two, without anything. Fearing that we've lost our connection (which wouldn't be all that unusual), I glance at Mu over the unit. Eyes meeting briefly—deep scarlet to Mayan blue—I flick my eyes towards the box as she moves to check the connection. After a moment of inspection, she shakes her head minutely—small mouth set in a firm line. No. We're still green.

At this point, the radio decides to crackle again, and the low grumble of the Colonel's voice breaks the stillness.

"Negative. Repeat. That is a negative Beta Team 226. Current SITREP incomplete for the sector, over."

I release the handheld's trigger, muting my end of the connection and pressing the metal hard against my forehead. A string of choice words comes to mind, but I tamp them down to be used for another, more deserving situation. Not that any of my team would disagree, but calling out your superior in front of the subordinates sets a poor example. That and I'm sure I would get my ass in a sling for it. I got to keep to my quota.

Though I'm reluctant to take on this assignment given our current state of resources, we don't have a damn choice. Beta-level teams like mine are charged with 'Clean and Secure' missions. Not the information-gathering assignments that Alphas receive, allegedly of a more sensitive nature. Each United Forces campaign lasts six months per team, with brief 2-week breaks between rotations. That downtime is spent repairing gear, resupplying, and receiving our next orders.

We're on the last month of our ROTO, so supplies are limited, particularly munitions and food. Don't even get me started on the maintenance our bikes are in desperate need of. Heat and dust are not friends of any machinery. I'm lucky none of us have split a tire or cracked an engine. I can't fathom what pulling a 180 and heading deeper into the dead zone will achieve. If I still believed in the Almighty being taught daily in Catholic school, I would send a prayer their way. I guess I'll have to rely on someone else to do that.

Venturing a glance at the others, the look they give me is grim but not deterred. That is just what I would expect.

"What do you say, guys? Feel like rescuing some damsels?"

Their wicked grins are answer enough. This assignment promises to be dangerous and lethal; ergo, it should, at the very least, occupy us for a short while. If we pull this off with all of our hides still attached, it could gain us some positive notice with the Brass. And, you know, score some for karma and goodwill, blah, blah, blah.

Queuing up the radio one last time, I confirm with Command. "Affirmative, sir. Beta Squad 226 will proceed to sector Zulu-Charlie and perform an SR on the Alphas. We can be at the coordinates within 72 hours, over."

"Roger that, Beta Squad. Base Camp One-Eight out."

Leading my team into a known, overly hostile region still nags at the back of my mind—probably somewhere around where my common sense is kept. It's not as though I don't trust my team's abilities as Zeta soldiers. Except for Rho, we're not fools, and I rely on my people to do well. This mission, though, it's not exactly like one of our usual cleanup efforts. A bit outside of our comfortable space.

That particular zone has experienced the opposite effect of other sectors over the past few years. Instead of seeing Zee numbers decline and dwindle, they seem only to be expanding. Not the typical pattern for their kind. The disorder usually starts small with only a few cases before growing exponentially as it overtakes the local population. On the other side of this crazy roller coaster, more Zee means less food, and less food eventually leads to less Zee. It's a wonderfully vicious cycle of self-destruction.

In theory, you simply wait for the ten to twelve months it takes for food to run out and their bodies to be bereft of fuel to burn. Without nutrients, the body turns on itself (and rather aggressively). Fatty acids and glycerol are consumed first, then body fat, followed by muscles, the largest source of protein in the body, and finally, the leftover human ceases to function at the cellular level as their mass simply disintegrates.

It's spectacular and well worth the wait. Even if the Zee are still staggering around at the end, they're relatively harmless in most terms. They can barely walk with no strength, making it easy to dispose of them. Not that I need things to be easy, but I'm also not going to complain.

It's a foregone conclusion—starve a living body, and it dies. So, why are these Zee not dying? What can they possibly be eating? Each other? I shake my head in disgust. Even their base animal instincts steer them away from cannibalism…well, regarding Zee eating Zee.

Have you ever seen a vulture avoid a piece of roadkill? It's like that.

The Zee are rife with disease and bacteria. Immunity from their mutation doesn't mean immunity from the myriad of nasty infections spread through the saliva in their bite. This is something that every good Zeta soldier is taught very early on. Either through paying attention in class or listening in on the tales of our more seasoned soldiers that are still active (there's no tiered retirement program for us Zeta soldiers, unsurprisingly).

Rho already has the team going through their weapons check and packing up before we hit the road. There's never a time when you shouldn't know explicitly which tools you have at your disposal to work with on a mission.

I call out to my demolition expert as her slim form moves between her coffin-shaped tent and monster bike while loading up gear. When I wave her over to where I stand, she immediately drops what she's doing and is next to me in a few long strides.

"Yes, Commander?"

"Do we have any maps of the area surrounding Virginia City?" In this, I do my best to be specific about which area I'm referring to.

"Topos, at least, Omega, but let me double-check."

I nod, and she jogs over to where her bike is sitting to search for the aforementioned info. While I'm waiting, I might as well get geared up too. The mail, vest, and jerkins I always have on, but the gauntlets, poncho, and shin guards are pieces of my outfit that I try not to wear continuously around camp if it can be helped. As much as the blasted armor is intended for extended wear, there are still limits to when it stops being helpful and becomes a pain in the ass.

In this day and age, layers are what is called for. Layers of lightweight but sturdy material that is designed to ward off all manner of physical assault by an enemy whose primary weapons consist of teeth, nails, and disease. Not an inch of space is left uncovered, save for my head, but that will come later.

As I thread the last fastener into place, I catch Chi's light footsteps alerting me to her approach as she gracefully runs over with two rolled-up paper sets and a notoriously fickle data screen.

"See here. The sector that Base Camp pointed out is the downtown area of the main city. From the East seems to be our best approach. There is a crescent hill partially enclosing that end. The steeper terrain will be manageable by the ATCs and for us to climb if need be. It will also double as an obstacle to any flesh-munching Zee that might decide to follow us out if we leave hot."

She pauses for a moment, running slender digits through pansy-tinted black locks in a gesture I recognize as fear. At least, as much as Chi ever invests in worrying about anything.

"What is it, Chi?"

There's a faint snort before she straightens up to answer.

"There is one major problem with the area—once we are over the rise, we'll be outside of signal range from any UF tower."

The corners of my mouth automatically pull down. That is not exactly what I wanted to hear.

"So, we'll be completely cut off from backup once we engage the enemy?"

"Affirmative. However, we have the tactical advantage when entering and exiting the city."

This is true. Even newly-minted Zee are less coordinated than your average Joe. Time deteriorates their muscles, making them even less mobile and marginally less of a threat. The only time these fuckers are fast is when they are fresh and well-fed. In the end, it still comes down to a numbers game. There will be more active Zee than bullets we have on hand, even assuming that the Alphas managed to take a few down with them.

"Are there any other routes that we can take to escape? I don't mind being able to see the enemy when we enter, but there needs to be a faster alternative for an exit strategy if it all goes to shit."

Chi's sharp features take on a considering expression as she rechecks the map.

"Well," she hesitates. "There was one, but I didn't think you'd even want to consider it. There appears to be some minor road leading up our hill. It's not marked on the map, but aerial..." and here she pulls out her gauntlet's data screen, no doubt calling up an overhead view of our surroundings, "...shows it is situated on the South end of the city's outskirts—possibly a service road or something to that effect. It would take longer to get there once we're within city limits, but it's a shorter trip up the hill to get back to our original position." She trails off lowly.

It's not difficult to decipher that, tactically speaking, she isn't happy with any of our so-called options. I'm not satisfied with them, but we have no alternative.

"Alright. It looks like we'll need to see this crapshoot for ourselves. Let's plan to camp on the South face of the hill and scout the area once we're settled in all cozy. We should assume that the East end will be both our entry and exit point."

She nods in agreement before adding, "I could also set up a few tripwires and perhaps a couple of explosive lines for additional coverage."

I can't help but give her a wary eye. We haven't had the opportunity to stop by a supply depot to restock in the last few weeks. She must be running low on explosives by now—we've been busy. Very busy.

"I have enough," Chi says.

"Enough?"

"Enough to spare for this. Not using my charges will not do us any favors if we are dead and gone, correct?" An elegant ebony eyebrow raises as she awaits my response.

"True, true." Ah, Chi. She has no fear of saying what she thinks or cursorily feels.

I glance towards the remainder of my team from where we've been hunched over, looking through the maps. With some small satisfaction, they're all ready and awaiting my orders. That's one thing that can be said for them—they may joke around, and some act short a few dozen marbles, but when it comes to the task, you couldn't ask for a better group of soldiers.

My waning confidence in the situation is given a temporary boost, so I nod again to Chi before explaining the plan of attack to my eager teammates. I guess one good thing will come out of this mission. Now there's an outlet for all of that restless energy that has been plaguing us. Let's hope it won't prove unnecessary for the job ahead.

Rho gives a loud hoot when I give the order to mount up. The others follow his lead in a slightly more sedate manner. Once my helm is buckled, I mount my ride and click on the engine.

The wonderful hum of its hybrid engines coming to life reverberates through the chassis of the bike, soothing my troubled thoughts for a moment. It syncs seamlessly with one of the UF's satellites as I remotely load the coordinates of our next mission into my bike's nav. With a kick, we're off.

SCOUTING AHEAD

The ride there lacks interference or chaos, which makes for a smooth trip. It's nearing sunset when we finally reach the large hill spec'd out at our previous camp earlier as a good observation point.

Slowing just below the rise, we cut off our near-silent engines. We should be just out of range and hidden from the wandering, vacant eyes below. One of the things that I have always found amusing (and I use the term very loosely here) about the Zee are the distinctly human mannerisms they've retained. The tendency to group and stay in one area seems to be a fundamental, instinctual drive for humankind. Rare are the times when we've encountered lone, nomadic Zee; even then, they still keep to a loose territory occupied by other Zee cells.

As an added precaution, my group's A and B teams split when we reach our designated position for camp. The bikes are laterally parked in a wide 'V' formation, enclosing our intended encampment and pointing downhill and away from our target if we need to make a quick escape. Mu and Omicron have already dismounted and assumed sentry positions, using their helms' built-in optics to scope out our surroundings. Their job is to ensure we're truly in the clear. Rho usually acts as a third set of eyes, but my team is still one man short, and Command seems to be in no hurry to fix that.

Rho, Chi, and I proceed carefully in a hunched-down form before crawling as quietly as possible, given the loose gravel and low, tumbleweed-ridden terrain, to a position at the crest of the hill and evaluate our objective. Through my helmet's scope, the landscape is lit a brilliant green. No fires burn in the town enshrouded by twilight below us. That says a lot about our chances of finding anyone alive, but it also makes it more challenging to pick out movement along the empty streets. From our position, the nondescript path takes shape as an unpaved truck road meandering its way up the hillside through a series of switchbacks. Not the most direct route, but a way in nonetheless.

I point it out to Rho and Chi to ensure we're on the same page. Making sure that we make eye contact, I gesture for Chi to stay put and continue observation. Rho and I inch backward down the incline like misaligned snakes before we reach the remainder of the team. Both look up sharply at our approach but say nothing. Crouching, I gesture for my two guards to join Rho and me for prep. Nothing I tell them will be new, but reviewing the plan of attack never hurts. Silence will be our favored ally here for the next couple of days.

"We'll sleep in two, four-hour shifts," I murmur lowly to them. "Rho and Omicron will take the first, Mu and I will take the second. Chi will be otherwise occupied in the morning, so I want her well-rested. Assuming Chi's scouting doesn't turn up anything new, we'll need to be ready to breach the city about a half-hour before dawn. I want us tucked away before the sun is fully up."

A glance over my left shoulder confirms that Chi is still in position.

"Chi will be moving about five to ten minutes ahead of us and will keep us appraised via Comms. I want a full sweep, left to right, front to back. We need to be thorough and careful."

All three nod in agreement.

Catching Rho's attention, I comment specifically to him, "I didn't see any tracks to indicate which way the Alphas entered, as well as if anybody exited. We must assume that they're still hidden within the city."

Rho's dark head bobs once. His voice is much mellower than usual in response. "I think they took the direct route—straight from the freeway."

A low hiss inadvertently escapes my mouth. That's a rookie mistake. More often than not, the best route to take into a town or city is the one likely to have been least traveled. Any soldier out of Basic should know that the complicated, multi-zillion-dollar freeway system that crisscrosses the majority of the now-defunct U.S. of A., both above and below ground, is one giant clusterfuck. A sea of wreckage consisting of abandoned, driverless vehicles and jammed transit tubes left over from a failed mass exodus of unfortunate civilians.

Gridlock was a death trap, slowing people down enough for their fresh and hungry pursuers to catch up. Those who chose not to abandon their means of transportation were left trapped for the Zee to pick off at leisure. It seems less likely that there will be much of our target to bring back to HQ if and when we find the Alpha team. If this mission isn't more doomed, to begin with, it's well and fully there now. If there was a god I believed in, I'd pray that we make it out of here alive. Shame I'm an atheist.

The crunch of loose rock alerts me to Chi's presence as she makes her way to my chosen lookout spot, sitting just outside the open circle of one-person tents. As she kneels at my level, I notice that the scout is fully geared up for her part of the mission. Instead of the standard poncho and semi-loose fatigue pants, she's wearing a close-fitting, full-body suit. The unique uniform calls out her specialized position on this team.

Chi has two uniforms—one the color of the desert and the second a specialized suit with costly chameleon tech that allows her to 'disappear' into her surroundings.

It's a worthy investment by the UF I don't begrudge her. I can't count how often her camouflage has given us a much-needed strategic advantage. It's advantageous when collecting intel on a Zee nest or getting the drop on those nasty motherfuckers is the priority.

Eyes never leaving the expanse of terrain bathed in green, I ask lowly, "Are you all set to go?"

Chi shifts her weight lightly in her crouch, poised on long fingers noticeably lacking by one and a half. The dull gray plating lining a forearm mutedly reflects the waxing light of a still-hidden sun.

"I am ready to proceed, Commander," Chi announces succinctly.

Nodding once, I give her the go-ahead. "Okay, then. Be back no later than 0530 to base camp." I don't need to tell her to maintain radio silence, nor the rest of the team. The last thing Chi needs is for her Comms to go off unexpectedly and announce her location.

This is a dangerous position for Chi, but I trust in my scout's uncanny ability to survive anything—like a cat, only less finicky. No, wait. She's that too. Hmm. Maybe with less hair? Regardless, there's no choice in the matter. She'll go in alone without someone to guard her back. We'll sit here in the relative safety of our makeshift campsite and wait. And boy, does the waiting get old fast.

Have I mentioned that, despite our rigorous training and abilities, Bravo teams are considered the more expendable of the Zeta teams based, as so prioritized by the United Forces? A dubious position to be in and one that I have endeavored to work us out of. To prove them wrong time and again through the success of each mission we're assigned and the additional ones we volunteer for.

This team busts their asses to get the job done, and it shows. I guess the gray area we operate out of is how we differ from other Beta squads. We do what is required to complete the mission. There have been one too many times in the past when, if we had followed a direct order, we'd all be pretty dead.

There's what looks great on paper, and then there's what works in reality. I think that's part of the reason we're hemorrhaging Zeta squads. Micromanaging soldiers in the field is a killer.

ENTERING THE DEN OF THE ZEE

I t feels like several hours later when a clear whistle breaks through my wayward musings. Instinctively, I hone in on the source— Rho. Once he has my attention, the gunner motions with his weapon's barrel toward the bottom of the slope leading to our position. Following the motion, I spy what he wanted me to see.

A slender form emerges from the surrounding low shrubbery and scales the shale rock making up the western face of our wall with the dexterity of a spider monkey. Her dark form melds perfectly with the lingering shadows of night. Mindful of the other two still asleep in our camp, I step lightly to where Rho is already seated and drop down to a crouch.

My scout ascends the remainder of the rise in no time, where the gunner and I wait to greet her. Sipping delicately at her standard-issue canteen, the lean femme pushes her dark hoodie back, revealing her long face and a set of tired ruby eyes. The grim expression on her face doesn't boost my confidence in our mission. I grant her a few moments to catch her breath.

Chi opts to make herself more comfortable, nearly sprawling out on the ground before finally directing her full attention to me.

"Chi," I intone.

"Commander," she dryly rejoins.

I give her a look of mild reproach before prompting her once again.

"What do you have to report?"

Smirking, Chi casually leans back on her palms, closing her eyes and tilting her pointed chin up to catch the first rays of morning light. She is the perfect image of nonchalance with a bit of impudence mixed in for good measure.

"Well, I can confirm that the city is a lost cause. There is nothing but corpses walking around down there."

"And the Alpha Team?" I press. Her eyes open in a slight squint against the ribbon of light cresting over the mountains. Finally, she drops a portion of her careless attitude and turns to regard me solemnly.

"I found five ATCs parked along the northern edge of town, smack dab in the middle of the main road." Shaking her head in apparent disgust, Chi continues. "I also found the remains of two of the team not too far from the bikes. It looks like one was their medic, and the other could have been a scout or a sniper." The lean woman pauses to chew on her lip and consider her next words. "From what I observed, I don't believe they managed to draw any weapons before they fell. What remains is difficult to ID." The last part, she says with a slight wince.

What a waste. Cursing under my breath, I carefully consider what Chi's told me. Their end was unexpected and not a pretty one. Any Zeta soldier's lives lost puts our numbers down and stacks the odds higher against our long-term survival. This team didn't anticipate what they would be dealing with, especially if they chose to enter the site head-on. It's an overconfident move that was neither by the book nor common sense.

I've had the perverse pleasure of running into another Alpha Team. There is a certain level of arrogance that prevails within these teams. A great deal of it is warranted. They've earned their rank, as you can't be on an Alpha team based purely on luck or who you know. I think it's human nature to become complacent about one's place and status over time. Inflated egos make poor decisions. Perhaps that's the case here.

Two confirmed dead and five abandoned bikes don't leave me full of comfort. This place feels like a "death trap," and I'm about to feed my team straight into its gaping maw.

My eyes again focus on the quiet scout, and I ask about the state of our local Zee population. It always helps to know how fast we need to run to keep ahead of the walking corpses.

"Well, that's another area of concern. Given the known timetable for exposure along the west coast, you would expect withered skin and bones, right?"

"Correct." I don't like the giant "but" that seems imminent.

"That's not the case. The Zee are still active, and there are a lot of them. Mostly clustered in small groups but still roaming about. Searching, I guess, for food?"

"More than we would expect to encounter, I assume."

"Right," Chi confirms grimly.

"Shit." My head throbs at the implications.

"How the hell did the Alpha Team manage to fuck this up so badly?"

"Poor planning. Too many Zee and not enough individuals with higher brain function and a rifle to properly combat them."

"Joy." Whatever meager hope I've been trying to keep alive in the murky depths of my black heart is gone now.

"There's no way we can take on an entire city of Zee, no matter how badly off they are," I murmur more to myself than the other two.

"Stop mumbling," Chi corrects me out of habit. If my eyes were laser-powered, she'd be a charcoal briquette. I receive the expected single eyebrow raise in response, and I rejoin with my own purely to stir the shit pot more. Unspoken threats no longer cow her. I need to work harder on that.

"Gather the team," I order with a sharp jerk of my chin in the direction of the camp. "I'll be there in a few minutes." My tone brooks no argument.

"Roger, sir," Chi answers, turning smartly on a thickly rubbered heel as she marches toward camp. At least she knows when to stop messing around. I wish all of my team were that intuitive.

This intel presents me with a minor dilemma. I can be a good little soldier and follow the orders bestowed upon me to the letter. This duteousness will involve marching my team into the middle of a hornet's nest on the very slim chance that there is anything (let alone anyone) left to recover. To endanger my team in such a careless manner is a useless act. But not to do so… Defying a direct order will get us court-martialed at the minimum. I've seen what happens to the disobedient in the United Forces. They're lucky if they ever step foot off a UF base after their infraction. Imagine copious latrine duties until the end of time. There's also the large target it will paint on our backs if Command believes we're at high risk of going AWOL.

Missing soldiers was a big issue at the beginning of the Zeta Wars. Let me state this clearly and succinctly; I have never disobeyed a directive issued to me or my team. Creatively interpreting orders to ensure things work out to my satisfaction? Yup. All over that. The kind of choices made in the field is seldom black and white.

My obliviousness hits me upside the head—five out of six bikes have been ID'd. There's a sixth bike missing. It's possible that someone managed to avoid whatever calamity befell the rest of the unit. A slim chance that someone survived the confrontation and is still among the few living creatures around. Assuming the soldier's signal is active, we can track it. Every Zeta soldier is equipped sub-dermally with a transmitter that emits a unique signal at hourly intervals. It can be traced by any other United Forces-issued medical device or vehicle, so long as it's within transmission range. It also serves as a unique key to most of our gear, particularly the guns and bikes.

Many Zeta soldiers have lost their heads, allowing scavengers to appropriate their equipment. The UF used to plant Zeta ID chips in the neck, near the top of the spine until that became common knowledge. Now they vary the location by the batch. Thanks to Om, I know mine's located in my upper right thigh, near the juncture of my pelvis. I couldn't tell you where everyone else's is.

Whoever it is, they failed to report to base camp, which I'm hoping means they've not left the area yet. We Zeta soldiers keep our bikes as well-stocked as possible with a myriad of survival gear and kibble. We're dependent upon them on missions and any time in between.

We must assume that this potential survivor has intentionally gone AWOL. There's no knowing at this point. No background or bio on the team was provided by the powers that be, which means I know fuck-all about who I'm dealing with. Perhaps it's not entirely unexpected. Since I've been a part of the UF, the sector we'll be visiting has been bare of Zeta soldier occupation. Unsurprising as it was written off as a total loss. I have yet to overhear anything from current base gossip to imply otherwise. They'll likely never be found if they are a potential runner, and we'll never know why. But if there's the off chance that someone is alive down there, it's unconscionable to abandon them. We don't leave our own behind.

Decision made. Now it's time for me to plot a way in, which we might walk away from later. Piece of cake, right? If only my luck was that predictably good. I must have pissed someone off in a former life.

DISCOVERERS AND DISCOVERIES

Soft chirping greets the predawn morning along our hill. Sparrows, it appears, are oblivious to the troubles of the strange bipedal mammals destined to scramble around beneath their wings.

As their lyrical singing continues, my stomach decides to join the chorus. At the same time, it announces my presence to all those who give a hoot. Half-consciously, I tilt my head to the side and consider how much meat I could get from one of those flying mini-chickens. I weigh the effort involved in killing, prepping, and cooking my unsuspecting prey and decide to stick with my morning MRE. Salisbury steak well done, slathered in some fatty yellow substance vaguely imitating butter.

Our intended destination is still cloaked in death's stillness, though I've yet to see a single lumbering, slathering Zee. Not that I'm a complacent fool by any stretch. Chi's report is enough to assure me that the undead outnumbers us, the humble living, by an unhealthy percentage. By some minor miracle, they've at least had the decency to congregate on the city's southeast side—well away from our selected entry point. With our knack for stepping into it, we'll probably find our missing soldier right in their midst.

Have I mentioned how much I despise this assignment?

With one last lungful of clean, crisp air, I don the upper section of my helm. The burnished metal slides home into the lower portion that cups my jaw as tenderly as a helmet of padded carbon fiber can. Securing the catches is purely reflexive at this point. The loose sand crunches loudly in my overly-sensitive audios as I quickly step to where the rest of my team is geared up. The priority is checking and rechecking everyone's setup. Here in Zee country, we always use the buddy system.

Rho's tall form strolls over and proceeds to tug, jostle, and otherwise test my armor to ensure everything is sealed tight. One more jerk of the upper portion of my gorget, and he flashes a tan thumbs up in my viewscreen. I quickly and efficiently return the favor, perhaps shaking him slightly more than is called for.

Pressing the 'on' switch manually for my Comms, I hail the team and make sure that I have their complete and undivided attention.

"Alright, people. Let's keep this sweep clean, heads down, and quiet. Our Zee appear to be lurking along the city's perimeter. It's the polar opposite of our position in the warehouse district. Of course, we know nothing for certain, so keep the line tight and check east to west."

"What exactly are we hoping to find, Commander?" Rho cuts in. "Chi says there is nothing to be found down there but a few new corpses."

Glowering, I answer his question, directing it to the entire team. "Intel indicates that there may be a survivor from the Alpha Team. Collect tags as we go for proof of death and see what else we come up with. We need to make our full sweep and be back at base camp before sundown. There's no way we're lingering here longer than necessary. Is that clear?"

Regulation helms are pretty useless for expressing anything that remotely resembles emotions. My team nods in confirmation. I turn to kick off our wayward trek. I make it just a handful of steps before something else occurs to me. Without stopping, I shout out the last order to my team. "If this shit spews over and we're separated, make for the exit point immediately."

"And…what about our orders?" Chi's quiet voice breaks in.

I can't help the smirk that grows on my face. "Fuck orders. If there's one thing we're keeping hold of from this crapshoot mission, it will be our heads. The blame's on me in the end. You got it?"

A chorus of "Hell yeah's!" answer me, and I nod in the direction of our fate.

"Alright, let's move out."

Our initial, slow descent down the hill goes off without any great catastrophe. That doesn't stop my stomach from turning in on itself. At this point, my innards probably resemble a roiling pot of spaghetti noodles. I do my best not to let it show. Sometimes you need to face the bull head-on and hope he has last-minute heart failure before you end up skewered.

It's funny how the dawn makes things seem almost normal. The bright light bathes buildings of both old crumbling brick and new-age glass with metal in its life-giving warmth. The number of recently constructed warehouses, spanning acres with their massive footprint, tells the story of a once-thriving commerce area. I can only imagine what this place was like before the outbreak of the war. Now, it's no better than an empty shell—what a waste.

I'd heard that some of the big eCommerce behemoths had bought up space in Nevada. The land was cheaper than other west coast locales, coupled with many open, undeveloped plots. This place isn't nearly as dense as Carson City or Reno. Not to mention, there's no way in hell we would be that far into the dead zone. My best guess, we're probably close to Eureka.

As we start our search, the more ground we cover, the more I don't want to be here. There's no neon sign stating, "something is very, very wrong here," but it's so apparent a hint isn't required.

Lower and upper windows are smashed out. Cars are strewn all over the streets as if some giant child played with them and forgot to put their toys away.

The air is surprisingly clean and fresh smelling. Clear enough of decay that I can pick out faint traces of moisture from the early morning dew. We are thankfully downwind of the Zee, so our chemosensors will pick up any partially decomposed creatures that come within range before being alerted of our presence. Here's hoping.

Near-silently, we slink along the cool walls and deep shadows of any available structure. The going is slow and monotonous, but it beats being ambushed. This behavior is not unusual—it's our normal mode when entering a Zee-heavy zone. The atypical part is that we're typically not assigned to this heavy of a sector. Larger Zee populations equate to large-scale operations involving multiple squads, arsenal, and tanks. Can't forget those tanks.

Each odd shape and unexplained shadow has my team on edge. We won't be caught unaware as we're presently far too trigger-ready. Hopefully, our missing soldier doesn't just pop out of nowhere—it might not end well for them.

Quickly, I hold my hand up in a fist before fanning my fingers out. Wordlessly, my team complies and spreads out along the edges of the roadway. A large, sharp-edged lump of something becomes visible several yards out. Carefully looking through my rifle's scope, I can make out an overturned ATC with distinct United Forces markings. It appears to be the only out-of-place object in the near vicinity.

Weapon lowered but still at the ready, I jog to the bike and give it a once over. What I find adds another weight to the scale, tipping the balance even less in our favor. The matte taupe finish of the bike— the same color as just about every piece of UF gear—is covered in fresh nicks and scratches. Some grooves are shaved clear to the bright silver metal at the base of the beast's frame. Its rider took a nasty spill that rendered his means of a quick getaway useless. It takes at least two of your average Zeta soldiers to right one of these suckers…or just one of little ol' me.

Rho shuffles to a stop beside me. His lead feet kick up a thick plume of dust, and I want to smack him. Halfheartedly, he toes the bit of material peeking out from its spot wedged underneath the bike. The rust-tinted stains are difficult to miss against the light tan hide.

Poor fool. The soldier didn't even make it off the main drag. That's one less of our people to find.

Sighing, I wave Mu over, and she perks right up. After joining us with a last little hop in her step, I drag her down to reality

"Mu, check for anything useful and collect. We're moving on in three."

Her blue-black locks bob excitedly with her vigorous nodding.

"You got it, Commander!"

"Omega."

Omicron's deep timbre sounds over the Comms, and I turn in his direction. He seems to have wandered off the chosen path several yards from our current position.

Slinging my rifle back into place, I walk briskly to where he's waving me over. When I get there, I'm kind of glad that I've just assigned Mu to a different task. Rho's lanky form wanders over after us, leaving Chi to cover both Mu and us. Dumbass. He waves a gloved hand ineffectually in front of his faceplate as if that will chase off the swath of black insects circling mindlessly before us. Beneath the writhing, crawling black sheet lie the slack-jawed, empty faces of the Alpha Team. Or what's left of them.

It must have been some time since they were among the living, though probably no more than a week. Their remains are overripe but not entirely picked over by scavengers. This place looks to have been their last stand. Based on the angles at which their bodies lie, they didn't last long—an entire city against a team of five.

Wait…five? That can't be right.

"Well, I'll be damned." Scanning over the desecrated bodies again, four, plus one more with the ATC wreck, I recall what the SITREP said about this team. "We're missing one."

From the corner of my eye, Omicron nods. Rho's shoulders slump dramatically, echoing the whine working its way into his voice.

"Great! That's just peachy. The guy couldn't have the decency to die here and make our job easier."

My eyes narrow, but more so at my gunner than in agreement with his words. I stoop to grab the tags from the first fallen comrade. The thin plates of imprinted metal are easy to find as their previous owner is a bit headless, the poncho torn to shreds. Fingertips sliding under the beaded links, I tug, and the dog tags easily separate from the remains.

Motioning towards the rest of the corpses, I instruct Rho and Omicron to snag the remaining tags.

The weight of the tiny piece of metal can barely be felt in my gloved hand as I flip it over to read its former owner's identity. Phi10. Another poor soul lost to the Zee. They'll hardly be remembered, save for some administrative report tucked away in an old filing cabinet at HQ, never to see daylight again. It's sad. In the end, this is what awaits a Zeta soldier. You can't fool yourself with aspirations of a long life.

We play the odds and have a slight edge over others to help us along the way, but ultimately, we all end up as the same bits of discarded carbon as everyone else. There is no rebirth for us. We've given our last life to live as monsters. Though, you won't find many Zeta soldiers who mourn this aspect of our existence. There's no avoiding it.

It seems a cruel way to treat your warriors. Whatever happened to never leaving a man behind? The straightforward truth is that it's impractical and inconvenient to recover our dead, so the ID tag becomes synonymous with our existence—optimum results through minimum resources and effort.

The high-pitched jingle-jingle of aluminum sliding against itself catches my attention. Rho's rangy self casually transfers several chains to our medic's crouched form for safekeeping. With that business taken care of, the now more complex and pertinent task is finding the missing member of this former team.

PURSUED

The first thing that comes to mind is to split up and execute the remainder of the search in all due haste. We may be able to cover more ground in less time, but that idea leaves me twitchy. I get a rather large and cumbersome sense of foreboding that splitting up is precisely what we do not want to do. Something about getting picked off one by one… Still, I weigh the value of speed over safety, as the sooner we complete this mission, the faster we can leave this place. Perhaps I'm just reliving past events, but this entire setup doesn't hold a good promise for us. It always comes back to numbers, and there are just too few of us to take that large of a risk. Orders or not.

"Rho, Omicron. Grab ammunition, rations, and anything else that could be useful from the bodies and bikes."

Not waiting for their response, I head for the nearest overturned bike and run the worn leather of my gloved hand along its sleek side. Searching.

All our ATCs are built similarly, but some have modifications based on their rider. For example, mine has an extra hatch installed beneath the dash, which houses a backup pair of handguns and various rounds for me. Rho was kind enough to modify it during a stint of downtime when he wasn't otherwise preoccupied. As far as I can ascertain, this particular bike seems to be standard specs. Three built-in compartments, the first of which wastes my time. Seriously? Freaking dirty magazines. So glad I didn't have my addle-brained gunner search this bike, the perv that he is. Or, God forbid, Mu. Yeah, that'd be worse in some ways.

The next two chambers are far more rewarding. A small stash of protein bars—of the fake-peanut-flavored variety—and a full clip of M4 rounds. Reaching under the dusty front flap of my poncho,

I fill up some of my vest's numerous pockets. As I straighten, I apply a little pressure with the heels of my hands at the lower middle of my back and receive a nice, solid crack in return. The boys are just finishing their search and seize. Once I'm sure I have their attention, I drop my helmet back on and smoothly lock it down. They follow suit without question.

The lime-green light from the HUD flickers across my face as the helmet engages, the Comms briefly crackling with feedback. The niggling sensation of something being amiss has not lessened. If anything, I'm hard-pressed not to check over my shoulder every few seconds. The specter of death is hanging over this place, and I'd rather not add five more names to his list. Jaw clenched hard, I war with the instinct within to run and not give this place a second thought or glance.

I don't want to go against protocol. However, I'm not on board with that self-sacrificing bullshit, and I'm sure the others would agree. My team is worth more than some random soldier who wandered off the beaten path—whatever might remain of them.

A low, sullen ping comes from behind me as I waver uncertainly between paths. Straightening immediately, I swing around to the source of the noise. Omicron is already down on one knee staring intently at something cradled in his large hands.

Peeking over a dusted shoulder guard, I make out an aluminum box no bigger than a classic, two-slice toaster. The dull, flat greenish gray metal encases a crystalline LED display. That fragile-looking thin, glass-like surface is deceivingly more indestructible than its casing.

Funny.

Shiny metal thingy aside, I inquire, "What is it, Omicron?"

By this time, the whole team's attention is focused on him as well. Brow furrowing neatly in the middle, he shakes his head slightly.

"I'm not sure, Omega. I'm suddenly reading a UF signal where there wasn't one before."

Rho harrumphs as he shifts his weight from one hip to the next.

"Well, that doesn't make any sense. Those signals broadcast continuously."

"Right, but it's here now. Reading clear and strong."

A glance from the medic my way prompts me to chew on this development mentally. Well, shoot. I was on my way to calling it quits and getting the team out of here post haste. This unexpected development raises an entirely new issue to dwell upon. There's one Alpha Team member still not accounted for, and without a doubt, this could indeed be them. It could also be a dead-end— emphasis on "dead."

Technically, without the electrical current our organic bodies naturally generate, an ID chip will cease to broadcast. The only autonomous, continuously transmitting device in our possession is the ATC. They'll keep going so long as their battery holds a charge, and with that solar skin, they could go on indefinitely. Of course, regular maintenance is required to keep the skin clean and clear of dust and any other particulates a machine attracts while plowing across a desert landscape—part of the 'other duties as required' clause of our Zeta soldier contract.

"Where's it located?"

Chi passes me silently, kneeling next to Omicron as she pulls up a projection of the topos on her gauntlet. The two compare notes before Omicron turns back to me.

"It looks like the warehouse district. I'll know better the closer we get to the source."

Lip sucked between my canines, I gnaw on both them and my decision. If there's even a chance this Alpha is alive, and we leave them to suffer the same fate as their companions... God, that one kills me more than anything. It also provides clarity to my resolution. Nodding once to myself, I take the plunge and commit my team to a half-ass plan.

"Okay. Here's what we're going to do. We'll take as direct a path as possible to the target. Single file, double step, and radio silence. Let's do our best not to disturb, and therefore engage, the natives while we're at it."

Chi and Omicron give me sharp nods while I get something akin to a shrug from Rho (who knows what the hell that means). Surprisingly, it's Mu who does not immediately offer an affirmative.

"Wait, you mean we're not going to split up to cover more ground?"

"Exactly."

"But—"

"We're checking this out as a team. Do you have any problem with that decision?"

My tone comes out sharp compared to the sniper's softer voice. I have little tolerance for being questioned, particularly when time is wasting away. There's death incarnate somewhere nearby, and I'll be damned if we wait around for it.

She shakes her head in response before her shoulders slump dejectedly, suitably chastised.

"Alright, if there are no more questions, let's get this done and get the hell out of here."

Taking a calming breath, I turn towards the empty road before us. Without another word, the team fans out behind me, each scanning for their target. My scanners are hot and ready for action as we walk briskly down the deserted main drag, unoriginally named "Main Street."

For once, Omicron is in the position at my left shoulder. The medic typically carries extra rounds for my gunners and lingers toward the back. He also wields a mean-looking M4, but in this instance, I need his biotech scanners, first and foremost, more than the extra firepower and CYA. Though he continuously scans the surrounding buildings like the others, his attention is split between it and the hand-held device in his possession. We're relying heavily on that antiquated tech to give us any UF signal or bio readings within a couple of miles—it should also pick up the missing ATC's signal when we're close enough, assuming that it's in the original vicinity of its owner.

We only manage to move in a few miles before careful Chi, of all people, startles a lone Zee. The creature just so happens to be shoulders-deep in a maggot-ridden carcass. A glance confirms that it's wildlife and not our missing Alpha guy. I don't know whether to be disappointed or gleeful. I guess the healthy response lies somewhere in the middle.

The point is that we're all caught off-guard. Enough so that the damn thing releases one of its cries—some awful moan ending in a high-pitched screech. It makes me want to claw out my helm's audios, as well as my ears for added measure.

Rho's the first to snap off a headshot—a quick staccato—at close range. It doesn't leave much from the neck up with the kind of ammo we carry—damage over precision, except in the case of Mu's primary weapon. Between the cry and the gunshots still ringing throughout the empty streets and alleys, instinctively, we hunch down in preparation for a shit storm raining down. With a quick visual scan of our surroundings, I apprise potential escape routes, weighing the value of getting to the higher ground versus what can be covered on foot.

The silence afterward hangs heavily for us all. Sweat gathers at the base of my neck before slowly descending my spine under the thick, taupe poncho. Pulse thrumming loudly in my ears, my breathing is a sharp contrast of soft exhalations. Maintaining a statuesque pose in a deep crouch while being poised for action is a bit painful. After more than a few minutes without incident, the tight lock on my muscles loosens ever so slightly. That is until all hope fizzles out abruptly at the clamor that my audios pick up in stereo.

The growing moans of the horde reach us at almost the same time that Omicron's bio scanner flares to life, picking up a cluster of pings north of our position. A lot of fucking pings.

"Shit!" I bite off the rest of what I was about to say. Cursing comes fluently to me, like a native tongue. Turning towards the others, I hiss, "C'mon!" Gesturing sharply with my head toward the most expedient path, and without waiting for a response, I push up from the ground, thick rubber soles gripping the uneven pavement and propelling me forward in a less-than-graceful sprint.

Screw stealth; we're moving now. Adrenaline and a healthy lump of fear propel my thighs toward their fullest intent. Heavy breathing from my teammates echoes loudly through our still-open Comms system. Ultra-sensitive mic's catch every little sound as we run full-on down the middle of the ever-loving street. We're in broad daylight, with no cover or time to care for what's ahead in the next thirty seconds. So long as it's not more of what's chomping at our collective butts, we'll be able to manage. We are being a special kind of stupid right now, and I'm the master fool in charge.

Buildings filled with dark windows line our path on both sides. I try not to let our harried reflections distract me from any potential threats lurking from within. For several miles, all that exists is the pounding of our boots against worn asphalt and the rattle of unsecured gear, overlaid with lots of panting. My lungs and feet ache equally from our impromptu sprint through purgatory, but thankfully being a Zeta soldier has some cursory advantages. Like a crazy level of endurance and a body that just won't quit.

Our pursuers have the benefit of not having any higher brain function, so things like exhaustion or frustration over a meal getting away do not affect them. A slightly harried glance over my shoulder confirms that our pursuers are now notably lagging. Maybe now's a good time for a brief intermission to stabilize our breathing and piece together a more complex plan than "run like hell."

A solid weight crashes into my side, lifting all 140 pounds of me effortlessly before slamming my ass to the ground. With the breath knocked out of my lungs, I catch a flash of decaying teeth as the creature climbs my prone form. Frantically it attempts to claw through cloth and flesh alike, spittle flying and hot breath fogging the thick glass of my visor.

Its straddled position inadvertently pins my right arm and gun underneath the weight of my own body. There's a nauseatingly close view of a purplish-gray, bare thigh in my visor as the Zee presses down upon me, pinching soft flesh between unyielding body armor. The putrid stench of a body gone septic permeates my helm and makes me involuntarily gag. Raw panic climbs up first from my lizard brain, and I struggle to get away from this half-alive thing. This predator that's doing its best to maul me.

I vaguely perceive the shouts of my team filtering through my previously ignored audios. I am unable to reassure their asses, nor have the care to. All my attention is consumed with forcing the Zee off and away from me. What should only be a pile of bones and sinew end up amounting to a hell of a lot more immovable mass. The more rational part of myself finally stops cowering, and I can focus on getting free and clear. Thankfully, my rifle is not my only defense. Not by a long shot.

With a concentrated effort, I turn my hips enough to gain leverage, using my lower body to flip the bastard to the side, as far away as I can manage. The quick movement lands the Zee right next to me as it tries to reorient itself and go another round. That's just fine. The size eight soles of my shoes dig into its midsection before I can leverage my back against the ground and propel the bag of bones several yards from me. An excess of strength may have been one of the side effects of my upgrade.

Before my attacker can right itself, the sharp crack of rifle fire fills the air, popping the Zee's skull with enough lead to put it down for good. Overkill much? I flip over onto all fours with a huff and sit back on my heels. Flipping my face plate up at the team, I can't help but snarl, "Really? We're practically in the black!"

I'm furious, but that doesn't seem to faze Omicron. He hauls me up like I weigh nothing and sets me to rights. Mu sprints over and joins us. Even with her UF-issued helmet on, I can still guess her expression as she radiates worry.

"Are you alright, Omega?" Her gloved hands are clutching tightly to her smoking rifle. My face screws up as I confirm with a suspicious glance that the other three have similarly discharged weapons in hand. They all fired, despite their ingrained training to do the opposite. Before I can berate them, the siren cries of the Zee echo loudly down the street. Only… it's from the opposite direction than where I expected it to be. The way we're running headlong into. I throw up my hands because really?

If these were regular human enemies, I'd say this was intentional. Like these Zee somehow planned an ambush. Where we've stopped isn't the best place to engage, boxed in as we are. We might as well set out chairs and wait for our markedly soon slaughter. My team exchanges a look. I'm feeling similarly exasperated and resigned.

"That's it! Come on—third building on the right. Scale up to the top. Move it!"

As one, we sprint towards the older apartment complex. Just a simple two-story structure, but with its decorative edges, it'll be easy to get us off the ground. Chi's lithe form rapidly pulls ahead of the others as she practically dances up the brick and sculpture-laden side. I allow a few seconds to simmer with envy before kicking myself into gear and using my particular abilities.

Rifle slung between my shoulder blades, I jump, and my fingers catch on an outcropping. Pivoting on a handhold no wider than my thumb, I use my greatest asset—brute strength—and propel my body up a length, grasping the next passable nook, not bothering with where to place my boots. The crunch of loose mortar to my right is Rho's long form. I catch Omicron laboring up a few feet below me to the left. Mu is the last to climb, kneeling with the wall at her back and making good use of her sniper rifle. The shots come rhythmically, one after another, after another, picking off the horde's front sprinters like bowling pins. As riveting as her work is, I'd rather she was doing it from on high.

There's another grunt and only 5 feet or so left to my climb. Chi's gloved hand reaches over and firmly wraps around my hand, pulling me up the rest of the way.

Turning, I shout down to Mu, "We're clear! Get your ass up here, pronto!"

Mu efficiently stows her weapon and makes the ascent after us. Her shots may have bought us a few minutes; however, she's barely cleared the top before the slathering mass of emaciated bodies piled against where we just were. Teeth gnashing and hands feebly scrabbling at the wall, the Zee are thankfully awful climbers and, therefore, not a threat for the moment. Given enough time and higher numbers, they will be.

I allow my team a few minutes to catch their breath and clear their heads. In the meantime, our original strategy has quickly become worthless, and I need to produce a viable alternative. Boots shuffling, I glance over the rooftop's low wall at the writhing throng of walking corpses below. Still not entirely immune to their general repulsiveness, I feel a sort of detached numbness as I consider the former citizens of a once-great nation. Pathetic.

Disregarding the Zee horde, for now, I pace the rectangular expanse of the roof—no more than a twenty-by-thirty-foot space. There are two exits. One decidedly untrustworthy ladder that curls on rusted hinges over the southern side and a padlocked door leading into the building proper.

Interesting that it's locked from the outside. We probably should cross that route of escape off on general principle. With a small sigh, I turn to Rho, mouth opening to deliver the bad news, only to pull up short. The open expanse of rooftops spreads out behind him, fairly even in their spacing—chalk one up to ultra-planned urban communities. In terms of ideas, it's not necessarily a really 'bad' one, per se. My gunner cocks his head to the side at the swiftly aborted gesture. Sort of like a bewildered puppy…only uglier.

"So, anyone do track in high school?"

The remaining team members turn to take in what I've noticed. Rho immediately folds over, head hanging low and sad between his shoulders. An incredibly nasal whine escapes what should be a grown man, "Awww, man…you've got to be kidding me, Omega."

I regard him with a beady eye. "Have you got a better idea?"

Mouth formed into a pout, he shakes his head in defeat. The remainder of my team looks equally assenting—well, as much as they can be. Rolling my shoulders in preparation, I bark out orders.

"Alrighty then. Let's secure our gear and get to it. No dawdling, ladies."

Needless to say, my team is less than enthused at the prospect of leaping from one rooftop to another for an unknown amount of time. I can't say I'm thrilled, either. We're almost to the midday mark, and the worst of the heat is settling in. It's hard to forget that our current stomping grounds are in the high desert. It's also summertime when temperatures tend to go well beyond 100 degrees Fahrenheit. We're bound to look like some pitiful, turn-of-the-century superhero movie—unrealistic computer-generated graphics and all.

A quick test of my chest straps, holsters, and rifle strap leaves me feeling good. Hopping onto the ledge, we face an endless sea of glass and iron rooftops. We've reached the outer edge of the warehouse district and all its grandeur, with row upon row of simple, now dilapidated structures. They're all built within spitting distance of each other, making this our best way out of this mess. Our fallback exit route is at the most northern part of the city. Hell, if my eyesight were just a teensy bit better, I could probably make out the line of C4 Chi set up last night as a precaution.

"C'mon, guys. Let's move out!" With a cry, I push off from the decaying edge with my right foot and land some yards away on the next building with my left—piece of cake. Chi alights next to me, all grace and stealth in one skintight-suited package. It's an interesting counterpoint to the other three thuds that follow her—their gear rustles and clinks, threatening to come loose.

And so we spend the next two hours surfing the corrugated steel. Bodies ache from the repeated push and pull of muscle and tendon and the jarring impacts against an unforgiving surface. I can't say this is how I expected my afternoon to go.

THE SURVIVOR

"How much longer do we have to do this?"

For once, the complaining does not originate from Rho but from Mu. Her body is slumped forward, helmet up, cheeks beet-red as she gasps for air. The sniper's cropped, sapphire-tinted bangs hang wetly against an equally drenched tan forehead.

"What? Do you need us to pull up a fainting couch for you, princess?"

My sweaty, raised brow is sadly lost beneath my helmet.

The sniper flushes brilliantly before her eyebrows draw down, and she responds, "Hmph! Not funny, Omega. We may be Zeta soldiers, but this is ridiculous. You can't expect us to keep this up."

Taking in her hunched-over form and the state of the rest of my crew, I may have to concede. As good of an option as this was when we kicked off, I can admit it's wearing thin.

Reaching back, I thumb the metal release of my helmet. With a deep groan, I take a full lungful of fresh air loudly through my nose and exhale just as audibly. Sliding a gloved hand through my sweat-soaked hair, I wince as a finger catches on a knotted snarl. Attempting to disentangle my hand from my head, I opt to reevaluate.

"Look, maybe we can…"

Ping!

A shrill ping cuts me off abruptly. It takes a second for my brain to kick in and recognize the sound. Almost in synchronization, my entire team turns and steps toward Omicron to check out the source of that innocuous little blip. The medic is already looking down at his specialized equipment with great interest.

"Is that...?" Chi starts cautiously.

Omicron's mouth withdraws into a line as he considers the display. It's a basic but adequate scanner—designed more for durability and practicality than usability. Without a word, he tilts the flat surface towards me so I can see what he's picking up. I'm no medic, but I do understand the basics of Omicron's bio scanner. It's a good rule of thumb to be familiar with my team's more specialized gear.

Lips pursed, I look over the readout, and even my untrained eyes can immediately tell that it's no Zee that's caught the attention of his device. Whatever registered is stationary but relatively warm... and close. Like, ridiculously close. Strangely, our scanners didn't pick up the signal sooner.

With a harried glance at our location, I realize that probably the only reason we picked up anything is our current resting position. This building is thick, solid steel but also missing a substantial chunk of its roof along one side. Standing in this spot is the only way to detect anything lurking in its bowels. In other words, sheer, dumb luck has found us our missing soldier. I wonder if that's the same for all of the buildings here. It would explain a lot of the misinformation that we've received.

Incredulously, I make my way to the ragged edge of the gap. No movement whatsoever catches my sight. Growling in frustration, I hastily wave over my sniper and, more importantly, her lovely scope.

"Mu, check out the interior and see if you can pinpoint our target in this mess."

The short-haired sniper nods agreeably, then easily hefts the mass of her rifle to run a search pattern within the warehouse. I swear if this is the remains of some Zee's soldier snack...

Doing a slow, methodical sweep for that errant heat signature, Mu is focused and precise in her movements. A complete contrast from how she usually operates. None of that overflow of bubbling energy—just sheer concentration and commitment to the task. A shame that she can't be like this all the time.

I do my best to remain patient and silent, but I'm too on edge. My size eight is about T-minus 5 seconds from tapping a show tune.

With an intake of air, she suddenly lets out a small "A-ha!" as she turns towards me. Her pixie face grins brightly before gesturing me over to where she's crouched with one knee braced against a splintered beam.

Carefully, she hands her weapon of choice to me like a mother lending out their precious newborn to familial interlopers. I do my best not to jostle, get dirt on, or at a minimum, not drop her beloved child.

"It's there. Right between those stacks of wooden pallets." Mu's slender, gloved finger points to an innocuous stack of shipping crates along the southwestern wall. She finishes her direction with another beaming grin before retreating a few steps to give me more personal space. I imagine my expression doesn't help. It probably currently resembles a toad that ate something it didn't like.

With the butt braced into the meat of my shoulder, I peer through the vibrant green glass. All it takes is one steady glance in the general vicinity to see the red signature glaring hot. Definitely human-sized. Also…not moving. That is not too promising.

"Well, I'll be damned," I mumble as I pull away from the rifle's scope. "It looks like we've found our MIA Alpha—and alive at that. Well, sort of."

I can't help the incredulity in my voice. With helmets now removed, my team looks as dumbfounded as I feel. Of course, Rho breaks the reverie with a loud hoot. I drop his joyful noise with a well-placed glare. His head tucks down into his shoulders, looking like some bizarre mix of turtle and scolded child. I do my best to ignore him.

"Okay then. Two lines, people. Let's make a quick descent along the southern side, atop those taller boxes, fish out our wayward ally, and then we can finally get the hell out of here."

Succinct nods and the team files neatly down through the structure's gaping maw. We edge down slowly and carefully. Just because the space appears to be enclosed doesn't guarantee its security or our safety.

The warehouse is dim and crowded with rows of stacked storage containers, now muted in color with rust and thoroughly coated in filth. Flurries of dust erupt into the air the minute our boots are down, but our helmets filter out that crap quickly, and our progress is unimpeded.

By the time we've reached the bottom, I'm reasonably confident we're alone. Nothing pings on Om's scanner, and the air is mercifully free of errant scents. Tracing the ground, it's evident that there have been no recent disturbances. I imagine our errant Alpha soldier must have taken a similar path into the building when looking for shelter. There's no telling how recently the soldier came through. I wonder...?

"He's here!" I hear Omicron's call from a few rows over. A quick jog brings me around the corner, along with the rest of the team. Once I've confirmed our missing Zeta soldier is there in the flesh, I redirect my attention to the others.

"Rho. Mu. Up top and diagonal. Eyes on our entry and exit routes." They nod and sling their weapons, quickly scaling a container or two above us.

Next, I address the scout, standing quietly to my left.

"Chi. Help Om as you can. I'll keep an eye on your six."

"Roger, Omega," she replies over Comms as she puts her rifle to the side in easy reach while bending to lend an extra set of hands.

Glancing at where the medic is busy scanning and running a diagnostic on his newest patient, I can't stop shaking my head. This is just too surreal. The waif of a man we found slumped bonelessly on the rough concrete is alive. Ignoring that he looks (and smells) like week-old roadkill, he should be summarily dead.

His team's last check-in was well over two weeks ago. Let's sidestep the obvious in that he's been in a city filled with innumerable ravenous Zee this entire time. Dehydration, starvation, and even hypothermia in this late-autumn desert landscape are big contenders for things that should and will kill you. So, how is this one asshole alive?

I suppose I should be thrilled that we managed to find at least one survivor in this shit show. The trouble is, now that we've found a living, breathing person, the onus is on my team to produce a mostly viable human when we return to base. That seems unlikely in the rough shape this guy appears to be in. The odds are not in favor of his surviving a 2,000-mile trip through Zee country.

Super. In the end, this could be another failing that Command will try to pin my team to the ground with. I don't understand why they are so apt to keep us from promotion. It seems stupid on their part.

Head cocked to the side, I try to see the Alpha past Omicron's ridiculously broad shoulder. There's not much to look at. A few curses are spat from the medic's hunched-over form as he runs deep scans of the guy, as well as poking and prodding him everywhere. The man is young, maybe late teens or early twenties. His facial features hint at some kind of Asian heritage, though different from Chi's porcelain visage for certain.

Hard to ascertain from his collapsed form, but the dude doesn't look as built as you'd expect from an Alpha-level soldier. Not particularly tall either, although that's another difficult thing to decipher since pretty much everyone left living is taller than me. I blame the water of my childhood.

The sweet tang of death lingers around his form no matter how much I try to avoid smelling him with my overly sensitive olfactory senses. I take a second to gauge through the skylight where the day is, but am blocked by a rafter. I can make out the sun's waning light through some of the shattered windows. We've been here too long. The trick is always to keep moving. Well, that and breathing.

I'd hate to spend the night in this place, surrounded by man-eaters with our bikes left out in the wide open. There's always the chance that some creep will come across our temporary camp and do their best to pilfer goods. In Basic, I once heard of a Zeta team that was held up three days longer than expected. They returned to camp mostly uninjured, only to find all of their ATCs' wheels gone without a trace, along with whatever was left unattended and unsecured. I'd rather not have an incident like that on my permanent record.

With the current situation as it is, I don't think we have much choice. Carrying the wounded will slow us down significantly. Zee are also markedly more active during the hours of evening and night. Something about ambient temperatures? I'll admit that I didn't pay much attention to the sermon—too many other competing priorities in Basic. This warehouse is clear and structurally sound for the most part. Our best bet may be to wait out the dark here and take our leave once the night melts off.

Decision made, I waste no time getting the guard rotations and sleep schedules hammered out for the team. We're old pros at this part of the mission. The only hitch to our usual rotation is that Omicron is most certainly off the roster. All of his attention is on the lone surviving Alpha soldier for now. That means double shifts and one tired (and invariably irritable) medic. Not much can be done to fix either at the moment.

After thoroughly examining the warehouse's interior, I determine that the best position to hold is right around where the Alpha has been holed up. The corner of the building has steel walls at our back on two sides and a maze of unscathed shipping containers stacked two or three high that nerveless fingers will have difficulty gripping. The taller stacks of steel shipping pods also make ideal perches for sleep. They'll allow for some forewarning if we're breached and need those extra moments of protection afforded by a lack of reach.

Waving Chi and Mu over, I direct them to the rust-colored metal that will be our luxurious accommodations for the night. I get two grumpy faces for my non-suggestion, but they comply. In the meantime, Rho and I need to set up shop. It's going to be a long night.

AN ESCAPE, HALF-BAKED

The slow, cool slide of something wet down my face is as good a wake-up call as any. Grumbling, I rub away the residual moisture and crack my eyes open slightly, allowing the waxing light to filter in. Far above, crystalline droplets of condensation make their steep, suicidal descent to where my face lies in wait. There's no way I'll be returning to a dreamless sleep now.

Our time is short, and the window to get our collective asses out of here will be a brief one. Through our accidental skylight, I can see the fading stars twinkling listlessly in the ocean of navy-blue sky. Their dying light tells me about the night's state and the fast-approaching dawn.

My body aches from everything wrong with last night, and I can't help the groan that escapes through chapped lips. The cold steel I'm pressed against unsurprisingly provided little comfort, but I've slept on worse. Yeah. The United Forces barracks are intolerable. I've got at least a few kinks that need to be worked out on some Zee.

I'm worried about the state of our new Alpha. Especially how lugging him back to the bikes will affect our exit strategy. Admittedly, I was hedging my bets between 'zero survivors' and 'kick-ass survivors who are ready to rumble.' Kind of an oversight on my part, as my planning may have been based on absolutes.

Leather rustles in the vicinity of my feet, and I finally take in Rho's still-asleep form by my boots. The short tufts of his auburn-colored hair peek above the collar of his poncho like a large and awkward burrito. Glare prepped for the morning, I aim a swift kick at one of his soles and manage to startle a snort out of him.

As I sit up stiffly and register the rest of my team, it's satisfying to see both Mu and Chi looking alert at their posts along the western and eastern sides of the warehouse. That only leaves Omicron. It doesn't take long to find the last member of my team. He's by the downed soldier, re-binding his arm in fresh bandages. Judging by the small rust-stained pile of rags a couple of feet away, I'm guessing that our Alpha is still losing blood steadily.

As if sensing my gaze, he locks eyes with me while finishing securing the new wrappings. I raise an eyebrow and nod toward his prostrate patient. 'How is he?' my expression says. He seems to consider, eyes sliding to the right before raising a hand and tilting it in a universal 'so, so' gesture.

Not what I was hoping for. On the bright side, at least the Alpha soldier survived the night. Our medic is brilliant when immersed in his work. The man is unerringly methodical and precise. I can't help but thank whatever god or Antichrist is out there that he was assigned to this team of misfits.

Gathering myself and my gear, I lay one more solid kick to my sergeant's motionless feet before crossing the space toward Mu's position. She's as still as a stone sentry at her post. Rifle up, eyes sharp and alert, I'm loath to distract her from keeping our glorious selves safe, but there's no other choice. It's time to make our final move.

A few well-timed jumps bring me across the last couple of gaps between stacks of crates. I land feet first with a soft thud right beneath the window sill the sniper is tucked into. For a brief second, turquoise eyes that glow faintly with an otherworldly light meet mine in acknowledgment before refocusing outside. That's all the invitation that is required. Easing up beside a leather-clad thigh, I take a moment to center my thoughts before breaking the silence.

"We need to move within the half-hour. We've already lingered here too long."

Mu nods and waits for me to continue.

"What's our current situation?"

Mouth pinched into a down-turned frown, Mu's eyes glance again through the single-paned window. "We're surrounded. They're mostly gathered along the southwestern face where it's probably the most accessible from the street," she notes quietly but noticeably lacks her typical optimism. "Chi's spotted a few stragglers in singles and small groups roaming along the other sides, but fewer in number than our main route."

I must be out of sorts not to have picked up on their presence. In my defense, this place already reeks of rot and death. Add to that a crappy three-hour sleep shift that left me not functioning on all cylinders.

"Damn. So, how many are we dealing with along the straight shot?"

"Probably close to two hundred," Mu supplies, sounding defeated.

Well, crap. I rub my hand down my face, anxiety and worry bubbling up in a vicious froth, threatening to overflow. With a shake of my head, I consciously try to slough off the feeling of hopelessness overtaking my higher senses. Instead, I choose to focus on the inevitable fight ahead.

"Sounds like we're out of options, but that's never stopped us."

I get a sardonic smile out of my sniper for my attempt at optimism. Grim-faced, I press the small, circular button no bigger than a dime located along my right jaw guard so that I can address the team.

"Okay, people. We're getting the hell out of here in 15. Please secure all personal belongings and half-dead soldiers. Chi, to me. Now."

No sooner do I call for Chi than one of the building's sides starts to shake ominously. How's that for spectacular timing?

Everyone freezes in what they're doing, all attention intensely focused on that wall and its overall stability. Beneath the hollow, thunder-like rumbles of corrugated metal being bent against its will, you can hear it. Scratching and drawn-out moans as thousands of fingers scrabble ineffectually against forged steel.

Unknowingly, the Zee are causing more damage to our shelter and getting closer to obtaining their prey through their sheer mass of bodies. A couple of hundred creatures bent on a singular goal are truly effective. Especially when that goal is cracking open the nut that is this warehouse to get to the crunchy, chewy center hidden inside.

"Shit."

That, for once, does not come from my potty mouth but surprisingly from Omicron's. I guess he was a little out of the loop with our current situation.

"Omicron, get yourself and that Alpha up here now! Rho—help him pick up everything and move. We'll sort our kibble out later," I shout at both men.

Slinging his rifle over his left shoulder, Rho's 6 feet, 7 inches of height are suddenly up and sprinting towards our medic's location. All traces of sleep and laziness are gone in the face of pure need and instant adrenaline.

Chi follows just as quickly, nimbly leaping from stack to stack above him, but breaks off from her path to join Mu and me. Grabbing her arm as soon as my demo expert is within reach, I all but yell, "Please tell me your side is clear?"

"No such luck, boss." She shakes her head to my utter dismay. "We're boxed in. They've surrounded the building and are seeking out that one gap to get in."

Clenching my jaw hard enough to hurt, those earlier feelings of hopelessness come roaring back in full force. There has to be a way. We can't go out like this—for nothing. Not when our goal is within sight and living another day is just up the next hillside.

A click from above distracts me from my tumultuous thoughts. Mu has her sniper rifle out. The long, sleek barrel is exposed through an empty pane in the window as she zeroes in on her first target. No doubt she's also marked her next three shots to take after this one. God, we've blown this to hell.

Huh. Blown to hell.

"Wait! Chi, do you have any more of your explosives in hand? Anything?"

I must look as desperate as I feel because her expression mirrors my mood at that moment. Cupid's bow pinched, she quickly sets down her M4 and pats down her vest. Each one she goes through that yields no results makes her grunt in dismay. It's a futile hope that there may be one last magic trick to carry us out of here unscathed. That is until she lands on one of the last hiding spots along the left side of her rib cage.

"Bingo!" she exclaims as elegant fingers hold up a brick of C4 slightly smaller than her hand. That and a remote detonator. I hope she wasn't sleeping with that in her pocket.

"I have one leftover from yesterday when I gave our escape route a silver lining." She turns it over once, contemplatively. "Although, it's not much. It won't be capable of destroying that entire horde out there, even if they were conveniently packed together."

Anxiety abounds as she throws the small package up and down in her hand in a careless manner. "We don't need to take out the whole horde. Just a wall. What do you think? Can you do it?"

Swiping the thrown parcel from midair, Chi flashes her pearly whites at me in a wolfish grin. "Can I? But of course. This isn't my first last-ditch effort."

"Good. Then let's open a channel as directly toward our exit path as possible. We're along the district's perimeter, so we should have a clear path. You didn't identify many additional structures after this area. I want as straight a line as you can give me."

"You got it!" She stows the pack...somewhere...before shimmying down the crates and heading back in the direction she originally appeared from.

"We've got a plan," I call down to where Omicron is hoisting the unconscious soldier from his splayed-out state to Rho's awaiting arms above. "Get your asses over here. We're running a Hail Mary play for the hills." The gunner hooks his hands under the Alpha's armpits, hauling him up while Omicron leverages himself to the top of the stack.

Once all three are on top of the nearest crate and Chi has returned, I lay out my new and improved strategy.

"Chi will create a way out for us on the east side. The minute she's punched a new door, we're going full tilt for our bikes. Chi will take point and lead us out with Mu. Omicron will follow with our Alpha. Rho and I will guard the rear. Once we've cleared the tree line, Chi will detonate the backup charges. After that, we should be out of this particular circle of hell, okay?"

I take in my team and their degree of readiness and willingness. Nods all around grant me total consensus (minus the unconscious guy).

"Alright. Let's do this in five. Everyone, move to the second to last row of containers by the east wall. These steel boxes should provide enough cover for us, right, Chi?"

She nods once. "Correct. Also, helmets and sound dampeners are on full, everyone. The blast can still disorientate you without giving the full concussive treatment."

All move quickly to comply as we jog to protected positions near the opposite side of the building. Slipping my rifle temporarily back to its resting spot, I unclip my helm from where it's been secured at my side and efficiently slide it into place, the eerily same motion at the same time as the other four.

After Omicron secures his own, he does the same for his patient. The bronzish-gold of the Alpha's helmet stands out from our grouping of drab sand grays. There's nothing like rubbing in the difference of rank, even though it's a moot point at present.

"Dampeners on," I intone to both my HUD's audio command and over the Comms to my team. Things suddenly become deathly silent. Even my fast breathing is muffled. It's as if I'm attempting to listen to the world through a heavy sheet of water. A bit disorienting at first, but we've had to run 'blackout' silent like this in the past. So long as you know what to expect, it's not as disorienting.

In no time, we're all in position, awaiting Chi's call. The burly medic has our target slung across his shoulders in a fireman's carry. Despite the extra passenger, he manages to look less encumbered than usual. It seems as though Rho has helped him out by carrying his M4 along with his gear. It's not likely Omicron would be able to make use of it during our mad dash, at any rate. Any equipment he can lose to balance out the 160-plus pounds of dead weight he'll be hauling is good.

At any given time, we're already carrying about 60 to 75 pounds of gear, from body armor and weaponry to those very handy basic toiletries.

Looking directly at Chi and Mu hiding behind the blue container across from us, I give them a thumbs up. They both promptly return the gesture. Deciding to do this gladiator-style, I turn my thumb first to the side before pointing it down. I have a millisecond to brace myself against hard metal before the whole building shudders and shakes as the ordinance attempts to rend it asunder. This must be what it's like at the epicenter of an earthquake. Dust and debris fill the pre-dawn light, annihilating its very existence while saturating the air in a noxious cloud bent on consuming everything within range.

My gear kicks in, and a moment later, my air purifier pulls in drags of filtered, cool, clean oxygen. Steroid-enhanced dust bunnies blink out of existence as my HUD automatically switches to a mix of night vision and infrared. The last of the rumbles are subsiding into dying echoes when the other two femmes of my team spring into action.

In sync, they lunge up and out of their crouched positions. Guns at the ready, they sprint through the after-effects of Chi's incendiary rounds. We haven't even moved before I hear the staccato of their rifles as Omicron follows them, racing through the remaining rows of storage.

Counting one second under my breath, I finally leap into action and take off after the others. Rho is at my heels, sticking as close to me as he safely can. Within a few strides, we're outside through a rather substantial rent in the warehouse. I have the inkling that Chi found something else hidden in her person to juice up her makeshift bomb. I'll have to ask her about it…if we live through this.

SUCCESS IN BITS AND PIECES

The first few yards are eerily still and clear of everything on the ground. It doesn't take us long to find the missing debris along with bits and bobs of Zee. I find myself either sidestepping or outright leaping over things I do my best not to mentally catalog.

Several yards beyond that, bodies primarily begin to appear. Not everything on this side of the building was caught in the blast. However, it did the trick in clearing our way. The bodies of Zee follow next, complete with well-aimed holes neatly drilled into the middle of their foreheads. Let it not be left unsaid that my sharpshooters hit what they want, when, and where they want to.

Rho and I are gaining on Omicron's position by this point. I can see his poncho trailing behind him along with the Alpha's. Narrowing my eyes, I make out muzzle fire from the sniper and the spy as they clean our path.

A roar reverberates from behind us, and I risk a glance back to see how bad it is.

Crap. Shouldn't have looked. It isn't good. The whole damn city is following our escapade of an escape from a crazy town. Can't focus on that. There's no time. We must keep at the task at hand.

A glimmer of movement and a muted heat signature flare on my HUD almost directly to the left of Omicron. Without missing a step, I draw my left handgun from its holster and put down the Zee. Double tap to the head. Two more shots fire from my right as Rho does the same. This pattern continues through the last mile of our dash. I can now see the hill approaching quickly. Won't be more than ten minutes at this pace, barring the unexpected.

I'm just gearing up for that last push when an out-of-place motion catches my peripheral vision, this time from my right.

What the heck is Rho doing?

The taller soldier waves his free arm like a fool to get my attention. Once he sees that he has it, he points to his mouthpiece. I try talking to him through the Comms but am met with complete radio silence. It seems my systems are down. Perhaps compromised by the blast. I tap my helm in reply and shake my head in the negative. He quickly flips up his ash-smeared faceplate, and I do the same mid-stride.

Cupping his hand to the side of his mouth, he practically yells at me, "I think I saw something we'll need that's a street over. Go ahead, and I'll catch up."

Not allowing me to reply, he flips his face plate down into place and veers sharply to the right, taking off down an alleyway.

What. The. Fuck?!

As I grind down, my teeth crack painfully. I can do nothing about it unless I want to abandon my position and leave Omicron wide open. Great. Now I've got to trust my interim second's judgment that whatever he's doing is worth deserting his post and team. He'd better not die. As nutty as he can be, I do prefer his hide intact. That, and I may need the idiot alive so that I can kill him later.

I can't say this behavior is entirely astonishing. Rho isn't the biggest fan of authority, but he's pushing it. Even with this rebellious lot whom I have the dubious honor of leading, they know better than to ignore direct orders.

My lungs throb along with my quads due to the strain I'm putting them under. Glancing up, I can see Omicron still plowing along, albeit a little slower than when he started. Regardless, the guy can be an absolute tank when it comes down to it. Makes me feel a little bit on the weak side for being the one who's out of breath but lacking the extra cargo.

I fight off another Zee—this time a middle-aged woman with a hanging flap of skin where the upper half of her face once was—as she swipes at the passing medic. I'm so close to Omicron by now that I don't even bother wasting the rounds. Using all my unnatural strength, I whip my rifle a good one across what's left of her fabulous looks. The result is a splintering crack and wet crunch, not so much caving her head in as shattering her skull and everything still attached to it.

God, that one will revisit me in my dreams later, along with all the other oldies but goodies. These real-life horrors are set on a never-ending repeat in my subconscious mind. Have I mentioned good sleep is hard to come by these days?

The big man suddenly seems to lose steam, and I have all five seconds to put on the brakes before I smack into his vast, occupied back (and more than likely bounce off like a gnat). With the rest of my senses now catching up, we've managed to clear the top of the hill and are no more than a few yards from our partially camouflaged bikes.

One more great thing about our ATCs is that they have built-in cloaking tech modified from back before the world consumed itself. It doesn't work when you're close like we are, but from around 10 feet and back, the 'skin' of each bike uses thousands of nanotech cameras to scan and accurately render their surroundings passively. And there you have it—near-perfect invisibility!

Faint, lusty cries howl after us from below. Even without looking, I can tell that what I've dubbed "our hill" is giving our pursuers issues, as we originally intended. Coordination is one of the first abilities lost to deteriorating Zee…right after their mind.

Bracing one of my gloved hands against the stitch in my side, I take as deep a breath as I can manage while cursing our lack of breakfast.

I take stock of the warm bodies I'm with and am supremely relieved to find them seemingly unharmed and functional. Omicron's lungs are working like a couple of bellows as I listen to him bring air into his oxygen-deprived mass. A 25% incline at a hard sprint is nothing to laugh at. I doubt if any treadmill I've ever been on topped 10%. It might have been a helpful addition to the base gym.

"Where's Rho?" Mu's voice interrupts the synchronized gasping going on. She's hinged at the waist, splattering the desert floor beneath her with sweat. As it is, I barely hear her question as she's facing the ground and not me.

Her words draw everyone's attention and a sense of realization from the other two. Oh yeah. I guess they would have missed Rho's abrupt sidestep. I attempt to reply but instead emit a squeak like a dying mouse from my radio for the trouble. Guess I forgot about that as well. With a solid whack to the right side of my helmet (which I'm sure is not all that reassuring to my team), I get that same squeal of feedback before my Comms chirp twice, letting me know it's reset and active.

"He took off before we hit the hillside. Said that he saw something useful, but frankly, I have no idea," I grumble. The only bright side is that my Comms are operational again. Chi was perhaps a little too generous with her explosives earlier. That, or she underestimated the blast radius and how close 'too close' was. It wouldn't be the first time. At least it was my equipment and not one of us that suffered the ill effects.

Scanning the city's outskirts, I do my best to pick out Rho's distinct, upright form among the slumped bipeds shuffling around.

Hopefully, he's not in the middle of the horde. If he gets himself surrounded by Zee at this point, he'll quickly be overwhelmed without our help. Maybe even with it… I don't want to wade back into that shit.

"So, what are we doing now?" Chi questions calmly.

Pivoting, I address my remaining team, "We stick to the original plan. Everyone mount up. We'll give Rho another five to get his ass up here in one piece."

Mu's helmeted head cocks to the side in curiosity. "Why only five?"

I stride resolutely past her to get on my bike.

"Because in five, Chi blows the line. Any longer, and our last line of defense won't be worth shit."

"But…" her voice gains a sighing quality, similar to a sorrowful five-year-old child. I'm not having any of that.

Barely turning, I stop her short.

"I said move out, Mu. That's an order."

I don't need to see her face to know I'm getting a look between pissed off and disappointed. Hurt feelings can't be helped. It's not that I want to abandon Rho's ass, but if waiting for him puts five soldiers on a guaranteed path to the grim reaper, I don't have a choice.

Chi swiftly passes Mu and me, heading to her bike at the end of the row. As I reach mine, my hand glides along its smooth side out of habit. I would be lying to say that my stomach isn't bubbling over with anxiety. A part of me wants to hop off my ATC and run like hell back into that mess. Find my second, whatever state he may be in. Hell, it may happen yet. The worst-case scenario is I double back after Chi clears the line while I send the others ahead. Strategically, not the best plan. However, sometimes the worst decisions achieve the best outcomes.

Climbing onto my ATC's expansive back, I feel dwarfed as usual. There is some comfort in that—even Omicron looks smallish on his bike. With the Alpha sitting propped against him, however, that particular detail is lost.

Okay, now we're stuck here waiting.

For Rho.

Why am I not surprised?

From our perch, the writhing mass below crashes against the base of our hill in undulating waves. Each one cresting higher up as the mindless creatures trample and climb atop each other for the chance to get at us. They're heedless of crushing the skull of the next guy or snapping a limb as they awkwardly shove by one another. Eyes rolled back, showing the whites and bulging red veins as they doggedly attempt to gain ground.

Checking my chronometer, I can tell we have just over a minute left before I give Chi the go-ahead. There's no way we can wait any longer, or our last line of defense will be a waste.

Mu shifts restlessly to my right, leather rasping against metal as her poncho and pants follow her anxious movement. Not a few seconds later, Chi behaves similarly, craning her neck to scan from one side to the other in search of our missing comrade. Fists balled in my lap, I'm torn between calling it off and going after my lone gunner or following my command. Granted, gunners are a dime a dozen in the Zeta ranks. Far more common than some of the specialized abilities each team longs for but doesn't always luck out in acquiring.

The numbers ticking by on my HUD aren't helpful as they draw my attention toward an inevitable conclusion. There's only a half-minute left now. 25 seconds. No time to hesitate. No pressure. 20 seconds. Ugh, I'm going to regret this, naturally. I can't leave the jerk behind.

15 seconds. No matter how infuriating he can be. 10 seconds. I'd miss our daily back and forth and his idiosyncrasies.

I'm leaning forward to kick my bike into gear and inform the others of my choice when I catch a dim roar that grows in magnitude. The foreign sound stands out against all of the organic noise below. The commotion starts to gain notice within the Zee horde, as one by one, they turn towards the approaching din. Sitting up as tall as I can in the saddle, I call up the zoom function in my visor. A series of taps to my temple toggles the setting until I can see a clearly defined plume of dirty smoke trailing through the streets of the still-smoldering warehouse district.

The cloud-causing entity barrels straight towards the Zee clumped at the base of our hill. It's nearly on top of them when I get a clear view of matte black steel and bronze detailing. Astride the new monster bike is none other than Rho. He gives a great hoot of excitement that echoes through our Comms, followed by a very distinct "Yee-haw!"

Okay, he's fine. I can now kill him guilt-free.

Instead of taking the less direct path and going wide around the mass of decaying bodies, he turns up the throttle and pushes the ATC to max velocity. The result is a spectacular plowing of the field. The arrowhead-like front of the bike carves a neat path through the creatures, pushing and flinging them out of Rho's way. I can only imagine the carnage that's being left in his wake. The two-wheeled superbike handles the steep terrain of our exit path easily. Modified tank treads catch and churn through the brittle, hard-packed ground right toward us.

With a great flourish, he clears the top of the bowl, gaining air as he does so—not an easy feat with the massive weight he's driving. Rho slides to a halt no more than a few feet from our line, the sudden stop likely giving his long spine a slight case of whiplash.

Killing the power, the auburn-haired man pulls his helm off—a mad grin fixed firmly in place beneath it. Through what is undoubtedly a huge rush of adrenaline, he all but yells at me, "Ha! See, I told you I saw something useful."

His overall enthusiasm could be considered contagious if I weren't so pissed that he almost cost us the mission. Before I dwell on his general lack of common sense, I remove my helm. The insulated helmet releases my head with a sickening squelch of moisture. Without pause, I ignore Rho and turn toward the mildly amused demolition expert beside me.

"Chi, blow it."

"Wait. What…?"

The rest of what Rho says is lost in the cacophony of explosions that take place directly behind him. After Chi enters the kill sequence into her left gauntlet's computer, chaos reigns. It's an impressive firestorm to behold. She spared no expense—or ordnance, for that matter. The sandy tan of the hill trembles before the face completely disconnects and slides in a grand torrent toward our would-be slathering admirers.

"Oooh!" Mu coos. Her visor is pulled back, bearing vibrant blue eyes that contrast sharply with the red and orange flame ribbons shooting up into the space surrounding us. I'm inclined to agree.

The aftershocks continue for several more minutes, lessening to a dull rumble before they finally peter out, leaving the city's outskirts draped in stillness. The now unmistakably familiar scent of charred cloth, flesh, and bone waft up along the rising current of air, leaving no doubt as to the state of the Zee. I feel a satisfied, albeit tired, grin stretch across my face. There's more than likely nothing left moving of this horde. As one, we all sit taller in our seats and take in the net result of Chi's handiwork and my damn good exit strategy.

All along the 'bowl' of our hill, dirty mounds of indescribable things and unmentionables fume, releasing miniature charcoal-gray clouds. Almost everything is kissed black from the explosion, including the two rows of warehouse buildings closest to the hillside. Now, this is one of the few things that I can still find joy in, as messed up as I imagine that is. Very few pleasures are left in my world, so I've learned to retrain my mind to accept what it can. Adaptation, after all, is one of humankind's greatest assets. Even now. Especially now.

Five of ours are now confirmed dead, but with one potentially staying alive and a mess of the enemy eradicated, it's not too bad of a day.

Giving myself a quick mental shake, I switch my focus to the present and the immediate future. Whistling sharply to gain my team's attention, I spin my pointer finger in a circular 'round-it-up' motion.

"Let's get going, people."

That soundwave will reach whatever Zee are still crawling around nearby, so it's best not to linger. Getting out of one situation by the skin of my teeth is all the stress I need for one day. Hell, one month. No point looking for an encore.

"Rho, secure the Alpha's bike to yours and take up a position at the end of the line. Chi, take point. We're moving to our next set of coordinates to camp, so we've got a good couple hours' ride to put in."

Everyone nods in agreement before settling back on their bikes and securing their gear. I've no more than reached up to seal my helmet when Rho pulls up beside me. An involuntary twitch starts in my right eye as I wait for whatever brilliance he's decided to subject me with. Grinning lazily, he leans back in the saddle, crossing his arms behind his head. His tall, lanky form exudes cockiness, and it takes all of my splintering self-control not to cave his skull in. Not that it would do much harm.

I grace his unmasked face with a lizard eye from the side as I snap out, "What?"

"Sooo...? Who did a good job, eh?" He drags out the first word with a lazy smirk.

In a flash, my gloved hand connects with the back of his skull, throwing him forward into his bike. The resounding smack that follows my arm's movement is very satisfying. I allow the little smirk I wore to drop into a full-fledged glower.

"What the fuck were you thinking? Seriously! Breaking line and running off in the middle of that shitfest? I should hang you up by your goatee and leave you for the next horde to chomp on."

His face droops. "Wait, that's not what I meant!"

He looks wrecked, not in a good way, hand bracing a freshly bruised cheek like an affronted waif.

Giving a begrudging sniff, he closes up his helm and obediently putters to the end of the line. Once the fool is out of sight, I give into the sigh of relief I've been firmly tamping down.

Finally, I have the time and presence of mind to take in our secured Alpha. Gaze drawn to the medic beside me, I make eye contact with Omicron as he offers me a quiet smile echoing my satisfaction. High cheekbones stand out in a heart-shaped face that's a deep tan, like all of ours—unavoidable when you're out in the desert country day in and day out. Besides the fact that there's probably not a single practicing dermatologist left alive, no one in this crew seems overly concerned with the long-term effects of excessive sun exposure. Well, except for Chi.

The Alpha has the distinct air of a classic GI, hair shorn short and neat, with just a couple of weeks of unintentional facial growth.

Overall, he's gaunt, scraped up on all exposed fleshy surfaces, and unremarkable in appearance. Never met him before, either at HQ or on the job, and I plan to put minimal effort into changing that. He looks unlike a lot of Zeta soldiers I've come across. We tend to be the low-rung dregs of soldierdom. I imagine he's one of those types with a remarkably pristine and smartly pressed uniform at all times. Makes me dislike him already.

Assessment done, I'm drawn to Omicron's pinched expression. It's apparent we're not out of the woods yet.

"Is he going to live?" I do my best to keep any trace of emotion out of my voice. No sense getting attached to someone who might not live past tonight, let alone make the 2,000-plus-mile journey to base camp.

The ebony man gives a deep sigh, obviously debating his next words. "He'll live. It's tough to say if he can bounce back from what's happened to him. Even with repairing the physical damage and rehabilitation, who's to say what kind of psychological trauma there is? That I can't help with."

Nodding both to him and myself, I consider this. Sadly, our line of work doesn't deal well with soldiers and PTSD. That area of the United Forces is quite murky. There's an ugly rumor circulating that unfit soldiers find themselves put down without ceremony or question. The same treatment as a rabid dog. We live in a pretty fucked-up place now. You can't invest the time fixing the truly broken things in this world.

Considering how much this string bean of a man has survived, there may still be a chance for him. It takes a lot for someone to live through a massacre of his teammates and complete isolation amongst hordes of unfriendlies. There's also the basic starvation/dehydration/hypothermia stuff.

"Alright, Om. Do your best. We'll take care of the rest." A hand on his shoulder is the best support I can offer before moving off.

I feel an odd sort of confidence in our situation. We survived this and managed to save someone. We'll have to wait and find out whether this soldier was worth risking what little we have for him.

ACT 3 - THE DROWNING SOLDIER

AN INCOMPLETE TEAM

With a final glance around camp, I feel satisfied with the overall state of things. I opt to enter my one-person coffin of a tent for the night, not bothering to do more than remove my vest, holsters, and gauntlets. I've learned that sleeping with gear still on is not worth it, but for now, I'm too exhausted to care.

My guns are the only items I handle with the care they deserve. As each is slipped from its holster, my finger graces the safety with a cursory check. Ingrained habit. Just like placing both weapons above my head within easy reach. I don't even bother opening my sleeping bag, instead performing a graceless belly flop on its squishy, pseudo-down surface. As my eyes slide shut, I don't pray; I wish for a dreamless sleep.

Now, there are those things…behaviors…from my pre-Zeta soldier days that have somehow still stuck around years later. Perhaps rooted to the very core of who I am. One of those quirks is that I can sleep virtually anywhere. I mean anywhere. Any position. Like a rock. I used to love sleeping in, you know?

This leads to my next lifelong habit. It's cliché, but I'm not a morning person. At all. About the only individual who can wake me up without a threat to their life is Omicron. He is the 'ready to go by 0600 hours' person. That might seem strange, but I guess subconsciously, I know he's the only one on this team I can trust not to do something idiotic. The other three nitwits are out of the question.

Mu always tries a little too hard to be 'nice' and 'helpful.' The second one, Chi, has an almost photographic memory, difficulty distinguishing between right and wrong, and a penchant for revenge tactics. Don't get me started on the last numskull. I'd just as soon put a bullet in Rho's forehead than experience his brand of 'good morning' ever again.

Therefore, it comes as no surprise when I'm awakened no more than a few hours later by a series of raps against the nylon-ish material of my tent. It takes a few seconds for me to dismiss the lingering desire for a deep sleep from my mind. Another two or so is spent considering the weapon I'm pointing unerringly at the interloper. Half-consciously, I thumb the safety back on my sidearm. Rubbing the cool metal muzzle against my sleep-warmed cheek soothes me in many ways. My jaw cracks audibly as a large yawn breaks free. I pathetically attempt to arch my back while still seated in a hunched-over position and sort of succeed. That's some raw talent there. There's the muted shifting of an impatient person outside.

"What?" I throw out with the utmost crankiness it deserves. Crud. It hardly feels like I've slept at all.

"Status report on the Alpha soldier, Tau, Omega." The quiet timbre of Omicron's voice rumbles through my tent. Fundamentally he's not a loud man, but the way his voice naturally projects does grant him that presence of authority…at least of the special, medical variety.

When what he's said registers finally, I perk up in anticipation. Finally, there's something worthwhile to come of this latest craptastic mission. Hopefully, his news is better than the last time the medic and I were able to squeeze in a few minutes to speak.

I throw on my vest, securing each fastening down the middle with cold, stiff fingers and half a mind towards it. The familiar routine helps my brain boot up the rest of the way. I opt to grab my gauntlets instead of putting them on as I turn and shimmy out of my tent, ass-end first. Once clear of the tiny space, warmth from the now unfiltered sunlight bathes my face. Eyes closing briefly, I focus on the sensation and allow myself to simply feel. Upon opening them, I finally regard Omicron where he expectantly stands.

His stance is open and casual. Thickly muscled, brown forearms are bare of the familiar taupe gauntlets I have in hand and crossed casually over his wide front. The fact that it's Omicron reporting and not Chi doesn't escape my notice. My medic seems more at ease than the last time I saw him in his entirety, shortly after arriving at our latest pit stop in hell. It appears he may have even gotten some decent rest between then and now too. The lines around his eyes are less prominent, and deep blue bruises no longer ring them. The copper irises themselves are clear and alert, reflecting a peaceful state of mind.

All of this adds up to one of two conclusions in my mind. Om either feels comfortable enough with the state of his current patient to leave him for a one-on-one conversation with me, or the guy's dead. I can work with either of those scenarios—I'm easy.

"Okay, Omicron. Let's have it."

With a long breath that ends in a sigh, he launches into an abridged critique of the Alpha soldier's current physical state. This aspect of Om I'm familiar with and prepared for.

"His glucose levels have stabilized, and all signs of possible infection are gone. He appears coherent and present, with no signs of cognitive impairment. However, he has not been forthcoming with any information beyond basic name and rank details—nothing that is not already known from the ID scan. I've held off pushing him for more for the time being as my priority is his physical fitness."

Pausing to refill his lungs, Om takes the opportunity to plant both fists on his hips and level me with a glare. "In other words, Omega, don't even think of asking me for any mission-related data. The guy has enough to deal with mentally without putting extra pressure on him."

The pointed look indicates that this conversation is seconds away from turning into a lecture. I mull over more of what the medic is skirting around rather than the spoken words.

"How's Chi's rapport with him?"

An exceedingly thick eyebrow raises in response. "It's fine. The Alpha soldier knows who Chi is and a bit about her role on the team, as she's been covering me for breaks. None of that matters, though. You don't get to use her other skillset on my patient. That's final."

"Why not? He's got his mental faculties and shouldn't be keeling over anytime soon. You said so yourself. It's also not like I'm asking her to expose his deepest, most maudlin thoughts. We need to confirm what happened to him and his team sooner rather than later. If Chi can pull it out of him now, I'll leave the dude the fuck alone to wallow in whatever personal hell he wants."

"You'll leave him be? Really?" His incredulity is unsurprising. I tend to pick at things until everything lays bare, raw, and bleeding before me.

"Honestly. If this guy doesn't say a single word to us the entire trip back to HQ, I will not complain. So long as he keeps in line and stays out of my way, I'll be good." I'm suddenly struck by a creeping sensation along my spine, as though some Zee has dragged itself across my future unmarked grave. I hope those words don't come back to bite me in the ass. With a shrug, primarily for my internal musings, I direct my attention back to the larger individual before me.

"Thanks for the report, Omicron. Can you do me a favor and send Chi my way once you've finished with her?"

His neutral expression abruptly flattens before turning into what Rho and I secretly call 'Mama-bear mode.' I throw my hands up to ward off impending doom.

"Wait, wait! I'm just going to speak with her for a sec before sending Chi on break. I know she's been pulling doubles with you. I want to catch her before she crashes." I tack on my sweetest smile, which is probably a far cry from anything sweet, but hey...I work with limited resources at my disposal. His thoroughly unimpressed look confirms this, as does his utter incredulity.

"Fine," he offers after a moment of hesitation. "I'll see you in a few hours then." The darker man gives a slight nod and vacates my space. Without a backward glance, his impressive figure strides confidently back toward his impromptu hospital.

Once his shaved head is out of sight, I let loose a sigh of relief. Don't get me wrong. I love our medic. He's just kind of intimidating when he wants to be. I, for one, am not keen on being on the receiving end of his ire. Again.

THE IMPECCABLE SURVIVAL OF SPAM

I stoop down and snag my rifle's strap before heading to the fire pit. Mu and Rho are already elbows deep in breakfast. It was probably prepared by the sniper today as Rho's cooking is typically of the well-done variety, regardless of the type of food. The guy must have zero taste buds. He could probably gnaw on a rock and be happy.

They're an intriguing study in body language. Both sit on boulders conveniently across from each other, leaning in as much as they can without ending up in the other's lap. Something I'm sure neither would mind, though probably not for the same reason. As I approach, I can make out the tail end of whatever deep and irreverent discussion they've been having.

"It's a nice idea, isn't it?" Mu chitters excitedly.

"Nice, yeah. It'd be great to be back to a fully outfitted team. Not that we haven't been trying to get to that point. Supplies are one thing. Solo Zeta soldiers in need of a unit and willing to be on a Bravo level one at that? Not so much."

"Yeah, but think about it. He no longer has a team, and we're a great team. We need another member for our squad, and HQ hasn't been in any hurry to fill that position. How perfect would that be?" Mu's optimism can be catching under the right circumstances. This isn't one of those times. It's an open wound that's never healed for the majority of us, and even Rho is cognizant of it. The sarcastic look he gives our sniper is a mix of patronizing and pitying.

"Maybe it's a little too perfect. The guy has been beaten all to heck. He's probably traumatized from witnessing his entire team slaughtered. Probably not the best overall setup for us to pull a shiny new squadmate from."

Rho's rationale seems to dim Mu's bright and shiny disposition for a moment. Difficult to look on the sunny side of this reality. I decide now's as good a time as any to interrupt. No sense crushing that sparse bit of genuine joy our team has been blessed with. The deep growl from the bowels of my stomach confirms this assessment.

"What's for breakfast today?" I cut.

Rho hardly blinks at my sudden presence, whereas the blue-haired sniper nearly upends her plate's contents onto the rust-colored desert floor in surprise.

"Omega! Geez. We didn't even know you were there. How about a heads-up next time?" A swath of mauve spreads across her cheeks and the bridge of her nose, joining a few errant freckles. My appearance has her flustered. Feeling guilty about something?

"It's Spam and GEGGs," Rho mumbles around a mouthful of said food, not even pausing in his meal to speak like a normal person. A ready-made plate of the stuff is abruptly shoved under my nose from who knows where. I don't ask about these things at this point. My motto is to accept and move forward.

Settling onto the ground between them, I dig into the lukewarm food. At least it's not calories disguised as food in bar form. I'd rather gnaw on a piece of granite and take my chances than choke down another MRE bar.

"Gegs, really?" I question after getting down the first few bites.

"Yeah, GEGGs! You know, Genetically Engineered Golden Goop. So…GEGGs for short. Doesn't hurt that it rhymes with 'gags,' 'cause, man, do these make me want to hurl most of the time." My tall interim second seems particularly proud of his accomplishment this fine morning. Sadly, this is not the first time he's made this joke. The next time may be one too many. It's not like he hasn't told it to the same group of people…over and over. Such is the wit that I get to live with on a daily basis. It's like being marooned with a younger brother who is indefinitely stuck at age twelve for the rest of your God-given life. Have I mentioned that Zeta soldiers physically age very slowly? Who knows about mentally?

"Okay. That's enough detail for me. You could have easily stopped at no explanation or specifics and been good." I wave him off.

"But where's the genius in that? How can we exist without relevant and witty acronyms? It's inhuman and inhumane to imagine a world without them." He sniffs over-dramatically, wiping an imaginary tear away. Now I'm going to G-A-G.

"A world without what?" Chi questions by way of greeting as she grabs the remaining plate of food and neatly folds herself into the lotus position across from me. She proceeds to munch away contentedly at her morning ration without comment while turning towards me for an explanation. Back completely turned to the gunner and ignoring him.

"A world without Rho's brilliant interpretation and butchering of what remains of the English language," I snark with an eyebrow raised.

"Wow. Say that it is not so," the demo expert intones mournfully, hand placed dutifully over her chest. She's the very image of a lamenting gentle lady.

"Oh, hardy har har. Just wait. Acronyms will be what remains of humanity after the Zee succeed in taking over the planet."

"I feel for the Zee," I mutter dryly.

There's a bit of pleasant silence for a few minutes as everyone does their best to enjoy an uneventful breakfast. Inner monologues are thankfully kept internal for the time being. As we're mostly all seated here, I take the opportunity to assess my team. They all seem better rested and less strained. Being stationary is doing everyone some good. Unsurprising, as our latest mission took a toll. It's difficult enough facing the enemy on an almost daily basis. Losing more soldiers, even faceless ones we've never met, adds another cold lump of misery to the soul.

Hmm. Speaking of our last mission…

"Mu. What was the response from HQ about our latest SITREP?" I haven't had a chance to debrief with her, so now is as good a time as any. There's not much in the way of secrets for my teammates. No point when we're practically on top of each other 24/7.

Brushing some stray, indigo hairs behind the arc of her ear, Mu looks anywhere but at me. I clear my throat when no reply comes immediately, causing her to start and finally make eye contact.

Playing with her cropped bangs while altogether avoiding eye contact, she shrugs. "They didn't have much to say. Everything we discussed I relayed to HQ, but they barely did more than record my statement."

"Really?" That's odd. Usually, HQ is all aquiver to get as much detail from us about a (mostly) successful mission as possible. They are also more than happy to provide their critique on any mistakes we make on the less fortunate ones.

The sniper straightens and swiftly switches from remorseful to laser-focused mode.

"Really. And that's not the strangest thing that happened. When I first patched in, it was with Carol as usual, but almost the second I mentioned we retrieved a survivor, the call was routed to some other woman. Whoever she is, she was more Zeta than civvie and all business."

"What did she want to know that was different from the usual?"

My head has tilted on its own accord. From my peripheral, I can see Chi and Rho paying rapt attention to the play-by-play.

"She wanted to know which soldier survived, their current state and if they had spoken to any of us. I gave her the rundown of the first two and informed her he wasn't in a state to speak at the moment. It was like that was all she was waiting to confirm." The edge of her down-turned lower lip pulls the long scar running vertically along the left side of her face from brow to jaw into a fairly taut line. Eyes focused inward, I watch her parse their conversation internally, seeking more clues to this mystery.

"I pressed to see if she wanted me to ask or confirm anything in particular with him and was cut off fairly quickly. She just said to return him to HQ, alive and with all due haste. Ended the connection right after that. I also never managed to get her call sign or designation. She verified her authority but disconnected faster than I was prepared for."

The spork clinks noisily against the melamine as I mindlessly shuffle the remaining bits of food along my plate. That does not sit well with me. My brain buzzes with all the implications tucked into this one infinitesimal discussion. Things are starting to line up in hindsight. The amount of risk for the mission, even for my team. A convenient lack of depth or breadth of disclosed information.

To begin with, they shouldn't have sent a single Alpha squad to that zone. An entire company, or at least a platoon, would have been more appropriate. There's something suspicious and mysterious going on, which begs the question of what. I guess it's above my pay grade to question why, but I've never been one for toeing the line.

I scrape up the final bits of yellow fluff and pale meat. The last bite is just as satisfying as the first. Licking my lips, I take a few sips of water from a tin cup straight out of the 1940s, more than aware of my teammates awaiting my reaction. The simple gesture gives me a moment to gather my thoughts.

Catching the violet-locked spy's attention, I tip my head, indicating for her to follow me when she's done. I know exactly where and how we can solve this enigma.

BAND-AIDS DON'T WORK FOR EVERYONE

While waiting for Chi, I grab a few sanitizing hydro wipes from the 'kitchen' and clean up my dinnerware. It's much easier than lugging the necessary potable water and a bucket everywhere we go. Bonus—they clean and disinfect better than soap and water ever could. Eat that, bacteria!

As I return my taupe-colored plate and utensils to their satchel, Chi casually sidles up next to me. She starts cleaning her stuff intently, but I know I have her full attention. I don't waste our time with shallow pleasantries.

"Chi, what are your thoughts about reading Tau?"

Unlike her demolition role within our team that she signed up for, Chi hates her obligatory 'other' part. The sharp features of her profile remain unchanged. Her tone when she responds is borderline resentful, coupled with an all too familiar underlying anger. She had no control over how her unique Zeta talent would develop, but she does have the choice of when she uses it when I allow her the decision.

"What do I think? Yes, of course, I can read him. Do I truly feel like forcing myself on some poor survivor's guilt-ridden soul? You already know my answer, but I'll restate it for the record. Hell. No."

With a harsh noise, she efficiently stows her breakfast set before facing me fully, hand placed precisely on a sharply jutted hip. Her voice lowers to a hiss.

"What are you hoping to gain from him by doing this? I know what the return will be for me—a massive headache and a sick feeling in my gut. Is that what you want?"

"You know it's not, Chi, but we need to find out what went wrong. Not simply for my sake but as a precaution in case we fail at getting him to HQ in one piece. I also need to know that he will not be a huge liability to us."

Her eyes narrow in either uncertainty or consideration. I've always had difficulty reading her, which is unusual for me. That controlled nature of hers makes her an excellent amateur shrink and particularly awful to play cards with. That and she cheats—I just haven't been able to prove it yet.

"That'll take more than one session, and chances are he won't let me near him after the first. Not if he has half a mind left."

"Then you'd better make this first-time count, Chi. Skim off what you can, particularly regarding the last few weeks, and let's see where it gets us. We can't take the chance that this guy is unstable enough to be a threat to us or our mission. We have a month or so ride before we can drop his ass off at UF headquarters, and the last thing I want is some ticking time bomb of PTSD waiting to go off."

"Way to go with the compassion, Omega. I'll be sure to keep my thoughts of impending doom and gloom to myself in the future. Hate to think what you might do to me." The smirk she gives me is not altogether nice and is saturated with disappointment.

"Oh, come on. More than enough crap has gone on over the last decade to drag any one of us down. It's no secret that we all have our issues. We're all survivors here; some use it to drive themselves forward. Others choose to give in and fling themselves off a cliff."

"Indeed. That is the powerful nature of loss and grief. However, we still must allow him time to accept what has happened and decide what to do with that knowledge."

With a sigh that deflates some of her earlier ire, Chi's tone changes slightly. Words taking on a more personal note. I find my mind slowing to match hers, and with a startled glance down, I realize my scout's supple fingers are barely brushing the bare top of my hand. Pulling away from her touch, my hackles rise at her taking what was not offered. Just as quickly, I let go of my irritation, realizing the point she's not so subtly making. How easy it is for her to ensnare and manipulate an individual if she chooses to.

"What I do is less of a science, more of an art, and that is being generous about the general unknown nature of it. My control is not perfect. If I read him now, I could irreparably break his mind, which would make everything that has occurred to this point moot. Regardless, if the Alpha soldier is reticent now, I imagine being used for information will not win us any more favor. Is that what you want?"

"I don't believe I need to give you my answer again. Nor do I need the morality lecture," I inform Chi shrewdly. "We have no choice but to put the mission, and this team's safety, first. Five lives have already been lost that we know of. I don't want to risk adding more of us to that tally. Take your emotions out of the equation and do your damn job."

That comes out harsher than I intended. This situation has me aggravated enough as it is. The additional body is another irritant, and to top it all off, I'm not thrilled with being an unwitting party to Chi's ability. Perhaps it proves her point more, but it's too late for me to change direction in my decision.

Eyes shut, Chi pinches the bridge of her nose. That's enough of a sign for me to know that she's going to do it. Personal values and morals aside, I know she can be counted on to do what is required.

Gracefully, she straightens up, lean arms raised high in a stretch before again regarding me with sharp, calculating eyes.

"I'll do this, Commander, but let it be noted that I completely object to it. If something goes awry, I am not to be held accountable." Without my leave, she turns smartly and removes herself from my presence.

The surrounding sounds filter back into my hearing as I lose the narrow focus my world has become. Rho and Mu are still chattering on in their loose circle of boulders, oblivious to what else is occurring nearby. Or perhaps not. It's best not to underestimate my team. The sniper can be incredibly perceptive of the emotional goings-on around her, and Rho is good at eavesdropping without indicating that he's hearing what's being said.

I find myself brushing my hands along the rough material of my pants' thighs out of habit before gazing at the barren, open terrain surrounding us. We've been here for too long. I keep expecting the Zee to stumble upon us. Just pick a direction. We're a tantalizing buffet stuck playing nursemaid to some useless Alpha.

Yes, he's the mission now and, therefore, our highest priority. That doesn't mean I have to be agreeable to it. Jeopardizing the lives of my team for one fallen soldier is not something that sits well with me. By assigning one, if not two, people to him, our defense is left with holes, and my team is doing double and triple shifts. Not the best for maintaining strong situational awareness. All I need is a reason to dump that Alpha's ass. Just give me the one.

I don't bother to say anything to the other two as I leave. They seem immersed in their back and forth, and I have no desire to get in the middle. For now, I decide to park on the eastern edge of our camp to keep watch and have a little alone time. An outcropping of granite will make a fine perch for my inner mountain goat.

THE WEIGHT OF ONE

Although the sun is now high in the sky and fast approaching noon, its spring rays are mild against the few exposed parts of me. Warm, bright, and thankfully yet to hit the drenching humidity I've come to associate with being out here during the summer months. Before those significant changes in my life and subsequently all of human existence, the furthest I'd ever traveled was the southern end of my 800-mile-long birth state. Not the most adventurous for a former California girl. Now I'm a sightseeing gypsy, strapped with an M4 on a never-ending road trip across the now-defunct U.S. of A. I would never have anticipated that future for myself as I sat in my high school guidance counselor's office, listening to him drone on about what I should do with my life. Also, never would have thought I'd end up liking a largely uninhabited desert.

I consider this insight as I munch on a pack of pretzels barely on this side of digestible. Two narrow boots interrupt my careless consideration of the dust beneath my treads. One pointed tip scuffs the hard-pressed ground as its owner shifts their stance. Following those feet along the long legs they attach to, I meet Chi's steady, if not disinterested, gaze. Her lean arms are all sharp corners, crossed with a hip cocked out in seeming boredom. As if it pains her to be here. I know better.

"Something that you need to report, Chi?" I do my best to project incuriosity. I enjoy a good verbal duel.

"Just a quick update on the Alpha, Omega. There's not much to report beyond what we already surmised. Don't get too excited."

I guess she caught the flicker of my eyes lighting up with interest. Hey, I can't help if I'm eager for any chewy morsel of info that she'll throw my way. Chi's extra 'gift' requires extended skin-to-skin contact and a certain amount of willingness on her recipient's part. The more open and receptive they are to her presence, the more of their projected thoughts and feelings she can skim off and attempt to read. It's a painful and disjointed process. From what she's told me, it's like trying to follow a five-year-old's retelling of a Dickens novel.

I twirl my hand, motioning for her to hurry up and get on with the specifics. Eyes narrowed, she gives me her best pissed-off cat look before giving in.

"No surprise, he's racked with grief and guilt. Overcome by it, if we're being frank, and he's suffering from some serious survivor's guilt. I'm not 100% sure about my assumptions, but from what I can deduce, he's more than likely the commander of the team."

"That would explain a lot about his reticence. Either shame or remorse. Maybe both." I nod more to myself than Chi.

"What about his mission? Was it successful? Did he disclose why his team was sent to that shit show of a sector?"

The sharp-eyed demolitions expert's fine features pinch together tightly. I can tell it has less to do with me than with what I've asked. A bit of that rarely displayed anger peeks out of a clenched fist and tightened jaw.

"Oh, he's a lovely ball of spite, resentment, and non-disclosure. The overarching theme I got was absolute bitterness about being alive, yet alone rescued and healing. Whatever his team's task was, it wasn't a standard clean and clear order or an accidental intrusion into that zone. They were deliberately sent into a hostile sector with no backup. Almost like a test or something by UF Command. Not sure what or who was being tested, though. His team had a good track record."

That's unsurprising news, as much as I hate to admit it. Easier to believe that those soldiers were an incompetent Alpha Team and not seasoned veterans.

"It also seems that mission failure happened even before the messy end that the team experienced. Tau would have preferred we had left him to his chosen fate as penance for his failure. That last part was his actual spoken words, by the way, and not mine."

My blood pressure spikes towards the heavens.

"That ungrateful asshole! We risk our lives bailing his scrawny ass out, and he holds it against us?"

The remainder of my snack drops carelessly from my fingers as I stand abruptly. My face feels full of heat, but that's an impossibility since my veins are flowing with ice. Without sparing another thought towards Chi or food, I zero in on the medical tent and storm towards it. This will not stand. I sure as hell will not abide by this behavior. Survivor or not, you don't piss on the team that saves your life.

Gravel crunches beneath my feet. Whatever the heavy tread misses scatters to the side like quail. A much larger profile seems to materialize out of nowhere, forming an effective barrier to the tent's entrance. It's not a surprise Omicron anticipated my approach. He more than likely heard me coming from Chi, and possibly even before. Particularly if he had any inkling that Chi was reading him. That's just fine. Squaring my shoulders, I plant my feet broadly to project as much authority as a 5 foot 2 person can.

"Move, medic."

The dark-skinned man crosses his arms resolutely, giving no way to my order. He's in full-on 'protect the patient' mode, and I'm having none of it.

"I said move, now." I bark at him. "That's an order!"

Om's jaw tightens, and his neck muscles bunch in preparation for a fray. Chin tucked down, I prepare to move him—forcibly if necessary. I'm not above resorting to using my unnatural strength. I can be a brute when the need arises.

"I won't kill the Alpha. That'd be a waste of the time and energy we've already extended to him. However, I will not tolerate your ward disrespecting this team. For the last time, Omicron, stand down."

Lines tense along his face, aging him temporarily. I wait on edge, counting to five, then ten in my head.

With one last clench of his meaty fist, the more significant man shifts, reluctantly stepping to the side and allowing me access to his domain. I continue to regard him coldly even after his acquiescence. He knows better. Don't question my orders; certainly don't bar me from acting as I please in camp. When our eyes meet again, I finally see some submission and maybe a hint of apology. That's enough— for now.

JUST A GIRL AND A BOY
IN THE DESERT

The rough canvas flap scratches against the careworn material of my glove as it parts cleanly to the side, allowing me entry. Immediately, the heavy odor of disinfectant assaults my senses. I'm positive that underlying all that is the acrid scent of various bodily fluids. This tent had been in use by the military long before Omicron inherited it, and the remnants of its past lives linger on.

With a nose as sensitive as any enhanced Zeta soldier, I find the aromatics here nearly overwhelming. I'm hard-pressed not to go and retrieve my helmet and seal that sucker as tightly on my head as I can. The only thing stopping me is the thought of having to undergo another face-off with Om while not appearing weak in front of the Alpha-level soldier.

Speaking of Omicron, I don't know how he can stand to be inside this tent pretty much all day without some heavy-duty air filter. It's horrendous. My only twisted consolation is that our new guest has been living here for four days strong. Speaking of which, where is that prick? The medic's tent is roughly a twelve-by-ten-foot space with no windows or natural light. This place feels like it's in a state of perpetual twilight, but you'd think the Alpha would stick out like some unwanted growth. As it is, I barely notice his presence in the dimmed light of the enclosure. There's a new cot situated against the far corner of the space opposite where I stand.

A few deep breaths of the damp air nearly cause me to gag before I manage to draw on some semblance of control. The being in this place is no more tied to this plane than those who've already left it. The utter stillness within is stifling and morgue-like. A sojourn for those on their way out.

Being close to the sensation of loss and loneliness emanating from the soldier lying prone before me is painful. Looking at the Alpha's shuttered eyes and drawn features, there is a shift within my broken world. It sparks something deep within my breast that entices me to mend whatever this hurt is. It's not pity, though. I usually have the emotional aptitude of a bull with the same amount of stubbornness, so this is new to me. Such an odd sensation.

Rubbing absently at the imagined ache in my chest, I finally take the last few steps to sit on the simple, black metal stool standing on three mismatched legs next to the patient's cot. He doesn't so much as twitch at my presence, but there's no way he hasn't sensed me since I entered the tent. Just another perk of the Zeta upgrade—a liberal smorgasbord of enhanced senses. I tilt my head a little to better appraise his still form. He seems young—no older than early twenties. However, it's difficult to truly identify a Zeta soldier's age as a youthful appearance characterizes most of our kind. It was challenging to tell what the soldier looked like when we first grabbed him and dashed off over the hill into the sunrise. Omicron probably thoroughly cleaned him up the minute his safe space was set up, per his OCD (it's not the need for medical sterility, no matter what he says).

It's time to get things dealt with. I'm done with silence, and there's no more avoidance.

"How are you still alive?"

The purely conversational tone I'm using may as well have been shouted based on his reaction. The man jars violently, twisting and turning so the canvas of the tent wall is to his back, hand raised in defense. He wasn't anticipating any interaction and my lack of respect for his sullen and silent mourning. He'll learn. Eyes as crimson as mine glare stubbornly back at me in a challenge. Now that won't do at all.

"I'm Sergeant Major Omega of Beta Squad 226. You're currently in my medic's care after an ordered S&R for you and your team. Care to explain to me why your recovery was worth risking the safety of my team?"

Expression closed off, the Alpha regards me with disdain, fueled by self-importance and what can only be a massive ego, in my unfettered opinion. His response drips with condescension toward me.

"I'm Alpha Squadron Command Sergeant Major Tau. My team's mission and objectives are classified and not of your concern, Sergeant Major. Quite frankly, I did not request nor require your team's assistance."

Seriously? My jaw drops as I grasp for just the right "fuck you" to throw back at this ungrateful asshole.

"Like hell you didn't!" I blurt. Way to go not reacting, Omega. "The only reason you're no longer in that death trap is that HQ decided you were worth rescuing despite whatever mission you and your team failed. How about being more respectful towards the people who risked everything for your sake?"

The frost in his eyes clears slightly. There appears to be genuine regret in his expression for a brief moment. It's gone just as quickly as his demeanor shifts once again into what I'm quickly dubbing 'pretentious asshole mode.' Sharply angled jaw clenched, he turns his head to the side like some petulant six-year-old not getting his way.

I've never dealt with small children personally, nor do I ever want to. I can, however, deal with this kind of behavior. Most soldiers I've met tend to be permanently stuck in their adolescence. I have to be the more mature one here.

"Look. Nothing about this situation is desirable. The fact of the matter is this here..." My arms sweep wide to indicate the tent and beyond,

"…this is where we are currently. You can't change the things that have happened to get us to this point and place in time, nor can I. To accept and move forward is all that any of us can do. Our priority is the mission." As you well know floats through my mind, but it is left unspoken for the time being.

His head remains resolutely turned away from my presence, staring doggedly at the tent's wall. I'm not convinced that he's heard a word of what I've said. I mean, absorbed what is being stated instead of hearing white noise. I release a sigh with the realization that, in the end, it doesn't matter. I'm not looking to make my new best friend today. This guy needs to understand his place as long as he's in our custody and my responsibility. Whatever he does once we drop him off gift-wrapped at HQ is not my concern.

"I don't need to explain myself to you. It isn't your concern, nor will I be once I am fit to leave."

Okay, I will not stand here and take that tone from anybody. My eyes narrow, and my voice lowers as I reach that place where authority comes naturally to me. Strength as a leader is not something that is assigned or contrived; it lies within those who are meant to lead. Somehow, I ended up as one of those people, ego aside.

"Like hell you will. I don't know if you missed it earlier or are simply incapable of taking anything into that tiny head of yours, but you are now my team's mission. Your well-being for the foreseeable future is on us, handed down from high. There's no way I'm going against orders to satisfy your need to sulk and wallow."

Lip curled into what can only be a snarl, Tau spits back just as vehemently, "There is no way that Headquarters would assign some B-Level female Sergeant Major to act as an escort for someone of my capabilities. Let alone have you and your pathetic team in charge of my welfare."

I see red. I'm sure my blood pressure is hovering around 160 and still climbing. Of all the arrogant, misogynistic, idiotic things to say when you're half-dead.

"We may be a B-Team, but guess what? This Beta Squad managed to do what your Alpha-level could not. We got out of there alive with a rescue in tow. Ergo, fuck you and your 1950s attitude. We're bringing you in as planned, or I'll be reporting to command that you've gone AWOL. I bet you're one of those guys with a spotless record that can't take that bit of red."

Eyes flashing, Tau's posture is ramrod-straight in his cot and glaring at me for all he's worth. Good. At least I've touched a nerve and broken through his aloofness.

My satisfaction doesn't last long. During our escalating discussion, I half-consciously noticed a high-pitched whine in the background. I initially shrugged it off as a manifestation of my increased need to kill, but that's not the case as it filters into the forefront of my mind more intently. Blinking away my hate-fueled adrenaline haze, I recognize that it's one of the many indicators hidden away on Omicron's patient that's throwing out an alert. Leaning back slightly to glance at the bank of monitors nearby confirms the same. All screens display elevated levels of something. Stress. Distress. Heart failure. I don't know.

Unsure of what's gone awry, the cacophony makes me reconsider the jerk sitting before me. Details filter in that I overlooked at first observation. Tau's skin is still pinched from dehydration, and there's an unhealthy pallor to it. Eyes that burn crimson are sunken into a shaded and sweat-slick face. There's a spark of life there now, but a lingering dullness threatens to return. His sheet has also slipped lower, revealing a shirtless and lean torso.

His musculature is distinctly pronounced, more than likely due to a lack of fat-padded calories from starving over two weeks. He's wrapped neatly in layers of bandages from almost head to toe.

The Alpha self-consciously wraps the arm currently not keeping him in his precarious upright position around his middle. That damn non-pity is back in full force on my end. Tinged with a bit of ol' Catholic guilt for good measure. Damn him, and damn this assignment. I need to get a better handle on myself and this situation fast.

The sound of stomping boots breaks my shaky introspection, and I quickly smother whatever feeling is trying to insinuate itself into my body. Tau's expression closes off equally fast, and I feel a growing dread that I've probably lost whatever meager opportunity I had.

Omicron materializes in my space, his bulk effectively blocking my line of sight to his patient and, subsequently, my access. I meet his fierce front with a similar amount of force. Before he or I can say or do anything to cause a real problem, I do the mature thing this time and physically bite my tongue before turning and exiting that tent without further ado.

HURRY UP AND STOP

My hands are still balled into fists when I step back outside. Breaths come so fast that I'm practically panting. It's at odds with the abnormally slow thoughts crawling through my mind. Habitually grinding my teeth threatens to leave a massive headache in its wake. I give myself a moment to fully embrace my vexation before consciously letting it go. After sucking in deep, long drafts of air for the next few minutes, the pounding throughout my body subsides.

There's no point denying intense emotions when you're in their throes. When you are this isolated from others, it's best to give yourself a healthy five to ten minutes to burn off any murder/kill/death impulses before rejoining what counts for 'civilization' around here. Honestly, I'm unsure what I achieved after that shared experience other than a migraine and jaw pain.

Yes, there's some validation of my theory that the Alpha squadron was at that site for more than just standard data collection and clean-up. But what could the UF have wanted so badly that they were willing to sacrifice a whole squad of one of their best assets? I can't hope for any clarity or specifics from HQ. They've been tight-lipped about this operation since we were first drawn into it. Something's not right.

My eyes lose their intense focus as I passively scan our base camp. There's not much to take in right now. Our low-slung tents are effectively camouflaged to avoid lazy visual detection by a stumbling cannibal. All metal is dull and darkened to capture stray light, as well as to prevent reflecting it. We don't leave any sign of ourselves behind either, whether from meals or ATC tread marks. No Zeta soldier worth their salt would dare light a fire at any time during the night. Might as well stick out a neon "All You Can Eat" sign and await your inevitable demise.

No, we can exist out here because we require very little to survive, and equally little marks our stay and subsequent passage. It's no different today than any other day roaming around in this oversized litterbox. Rho and Mu are assigned to the perimeter, at polar opposite ends of our defined campsite. Chi is getting her much-needed beauty sleep in one of the four identical taupe-shaded tents. Again, they are innocuous in design and easily missed with their low profiles and matte finish. In actuality, the medic's domain is the only thing that sticks out currently, and that's only because of its overall size. I throw it a half-hearted glare before heading away from it.

Right now, I'm left with little to do to occupy myself. I already recorded and submitted my report to HQ, laying out the trials and insanity that was our last S&R mission. I Slept. Ate. Yelled at the Alpha. Yup, for once, nothing requires my full and immediate attention. The trouble is that this rare free time that I find myself saddled with doesn't mesh well with how high-strung and pissed off I still am from my encounter with Tau. It leaves me with few options to diffuse myself constructively.

Releasing the sigh caught in my upper chest at the last minute, I stride over to my tent and quickly snag my helmet from inside the door's flap. With a quick about-face, I head towards the south end of camp and wave over to Rho's form at his guard position. Once I have his undivided attention, I slide the cool metal of my helm on and activate its Comms, queuing up Rho's private channel. Without waiting for a reply, I begin issuing orders to my adjunct second while finishing the motions of sealing and securing the helmet to the collar.

"Rho, I'm going to take my bike and do a deep perimeter check. It shouldn't be more than an hour. Let me know if anything goes sideways while I'm gone."

There's a click over the line as it transmits, then the slim gunner responds. "You got it, Megs. Have fun scaring the local wildlife!"

"Ha, ha. Fuck you. Maybe I should make it two hours." I throw an errant bird over my shoulder as I stroll toward the nest of bikes parked along the western perimeter.

Sliding onto my beast, my body's mere presence unlocks the ATC's systems as I toggle the metal monstrosity to life. With a press of the ignition and a hard turn of the throttle, my bike takes off with me along for the ride.

There are few things left to love about this world. However, I do genuinely enjoy riding on my UF-issued bike across what remains of this country. These machines are a marvel of technology. A sleek mix of old-fashioned tank sturdiness wrapped around a techie's solar-powered wet dream. Most ATCs outlive their Zeta soldier if that's any indication of how well they're built. I've seen these things flooded in river crossings, buried under rockslides, and even blown up with IEDs, and still, they stand in more or less one solid piece. It's a far cry from the outdated dirt bike I used to sneak out to ride on weekends with my sort-of high school friends. Not that my parents had a clue about either back then.

I quell my inner fangirl as the landscape flashes by and focus on the terrain ahead. Systematically, I scan with both my HUD and eyes for any anomalies. Although most Zee are not particularly fast, being neither sprinters nor marathoners, their long-distance shuffling can bring them upon you sooner than you would expect. The UF recommends keeping a clean perimeter of at least ten to fifteen miles around camp to be safe from potential interlopers.

We have low-tech warning devices installed along our imaginary perimeter, but I prefer my senses. It's not just the Zee that we have to worry about out here. Here is a reborn Wild West, complete with wandering gypsies, marauders, and cold-blooded murderers bent on making humanity's final breath full of blood and terror. And they usually have more than just their feet or horses at their disposal.

Remember that thing about embedded ID chips? Well, some particularly nasty individuals have figured out one of the many uses for them and done their best to exploit it. Some of our ATCs have been commandeered by precisely the wrong kind of folk. The butchered Zeta soldiers left behind are proof of that. I don't give much quarter to that particular breed of human. They're not who we're trying to save the world for, after all.

I can't help thinking about the UF-built settlements that have sprung up along the reclaimed Midwest territories. Tens of miles of sterile gray concrete walls enclose townships of survivors. Safe from the Zee, but never able to leave their high perimeter. Their only outside interactions are with the UF or UF-sanctioned parties. I'm not sure that's how to live, but it is how you survive.

The first half-hour or so of my ride is terribly uneventful. I sadly manage not to run over any random jackrabbits or pesky criminals. Minute thirty-one, however, is a different story. I slam down the air brakes of my bike and slide to a near-soundless stop. Matte gray dust flares up, enveloping me in a cloud as I brace the weight of my bike against one resting foot. Calmly, I wait for the mess in the air to dissipate while staring intently at the ground next to my rubber treads. Finally, the tension begins to leave my shoulders as nothing but earth and underbrush are revealed, and I'm just about ready to kick off again when I see it.

Shit. A bare footprint. Perfectly pressed into the soft earth right next to where my front tire stopped.

Helm hanging down, my headache returns in full like a tidal wave. My head snaps up to take a quick scan around me. Nothing immediately seems out of place. No evidence of an uninvited interloper. Yet, the closer I look, the more those human-shaped footprints seem to spring out of the fine powder. They're of varying sizes and shapes. All appear to travel in no particular direction, as if the owners of those feet had no clear destination in mind. Without a doubt, these were left by Zee. There are some things you just can't fake.

Marauders may try to emulate the tracks of the Zee hordes to hide their presence, but it's more than apparent when they are contrived. You can't imitate what comes naturally to a group of mindless, soulless people-eaters. I need to locate these fuckers and then get back to camp.

Tapping the side of my helm, I toggle through channels on my HUD until I've pulled up Rho's one.

"Rho, do you copy? Over." There's not even a full second of silence before I get a response.

"Reading you loud and clear, Omega. What's your status?" Rho replies.

"I'm Yellow at the moment. Found signs of a Zee contingent around the 40-mile mark, south-southwest. Are you still clear at Base Camp?"

"Damn. Yes, we're still Green."

"Well," I start, "Looks like some friends of ours are going to be potentially crashing our dinner party. We might require a new location."

There's a second of silence before Rho replies peevishly. "You've got to be kidding me. I like our new digs!" He pauses briefly, then huffs out a question. "Do you want me to break camp and mobilize the team?"

I'm a little short in my reply.

"Do you have something else to do, Rho?"

His lack of reply is the only response I get. I can imagine him petulantly crossing his arms, as is typical of him. Nothing I hadn't anticipated, reaction-wise.

Chi's smooth voice breaks in unexpectedly. "So, what exactly are we facing?"

She must have been close enough to overhear his speakers. With a deep exhale, I let my posture slump for a moment before laying out the facts.

"It looks like a good-sized horde. I can't tell what numbers we're looking at. I have yet to lay eyes on the real mass, but I estimate around fifty bodies. I can't confirm if they're following our trail or if we happen to be aligned with their feeding path."

Omicron's deep rumble joins the other two on the Comms. "And our next course of action is what, Omega? I have a patient that still can't be safely moved at this point."

"Isn't that just the core of our problem? Look, Omicron." I begin, exasperated. "All that you've done until this point isn't going to matter if the Alpha is torn apart by a hungry pack of Zee, along with the rest of us, right? Our best option is to pack up and hightail our asses out of here rather than sit idly by and pray we don't get slaughtered."

My medic may continue to challenge my decision, but in the end, he doesn't get a say in this matter, and he knows it.

"Look, we're not in a good position here. It's too open. We need to find a more defensible space, and at the very least, moving inland towards the mountains gives us time to consider our options. You then have my permission to heal the Alpha at your own speed."

Without an immediate rejoinder from Omicron, I can imagine him standing there, arms crossed and head tucked down, methodically working through different scenarios before coming to a decision.

"All right," Omicron finally consents. "I guess that's what we've got to do. He'll be okay for a short move, but nothing beyond that."

"Good. That's what we have to do. I want everyone ready to relocate within two hours from now. Clear?"

"Crystal," Mu chimes in as the other three agree.

"Mu, you have the least amount of crap to gather. Can you help Om get the medical tent and his precious patient situated? I need you to be the eyes in the back of his head. He's going to need them."

"Righty-o, Commander! The two of us can have everything ready in no time." I can imagine her glittering smile. Ugh.

"Alright then." I snap off. Switching over to a private frequency, I solely hail my de facto second.

"Rho, can you take care of my tent and gear? There shouldn't be much to pack, but I may not have the time."

Thankfully we live a solitary and nomadic life, so material possessions are something we don't have to concern ourselves with. Roughly translated, that means I haven't got shit. The most personal items I've held onto are kept in a marginally dented tin box held closed by a rubber band. Rho is intimately familiar with it, but I expect he'll respect my stuff in this situation.

"It's not a problem, Megs." There's no trace of humor in Rho's tone. He's a good soldier when the time calls for it. "Are you headin' back now, then?"

"Negative, Rho. I'm going to pursue this lead and see if I can put a current location and accurate size estimate on this cell. Make sure everyone is ready, but no sense freaking out yet."

"Copy that, boss. I'll make sure that we're ready and willing."

My gunner's voice is solid and efficient over the line. As much of an annoyance as he tends to be, I can count on Rho to be my rock when things start to go to hell, as they often do. I guess it's not all that charitable of me to complain about him as much as I do. But as they say, this is this, and that is that. So long as I know Rho is there for me, and I am for him when it counts, it doesn't matter.

"Roger that. I'll check back in 20 or so and let you know what I've found."

"K. Keep safe, Megs!"

SURROUNDED

I don't wait for Rho to sign off before I shut down my Comms, releasing the bike's throttle and killing the rumble of my beast. These tracks are fresh, and I stand a better chance of not alerting the Zee to my presence if I'm on foot. I quickly slide off and lock down the ATC. As quiet as the desert can be, this is ridiculous.

It's still of life. Something came through here recently that reeked of wrong, and nature took note of it. I pull my rifle around with its shoulder strap until it sits primly at the ready and flick the safety off. I finger the trigger for a moment as I contemplate my surroundings. One more glance towards the ground gives me a direction to go. With light steps, I follow that broken trail.

Is it truly my best logic to venture off after an unknown enemy without some kind of backup? Probably not. However, the alternative is unacceptable. I'm not wasting my time running back to camp, getting my team assembled and ready, followed by a redistribution of orders and people, then finally making my way back to this precise location with backup in tow. All under the hope that this unknown cell is still hanging out somewhere nearby, awaiting our imminent return. Yeah. Not a realistic option.

At a brisk jog, I do my best to trace the mess of prints embossed into the ground. Just looking at them makes my head hurt, but I can tell that their sideways square dance seems to be at least progressing in the same general direction. Whatever drives their march, it's strong enough to keep the horde together and moving as a single-minded unit.

The low thuds of my boots connecting with the hard-pressed earth are hardly audible, but I feel their sound carry just the same. The enhanced audio tuners of my helm only help to magnify the amount of noise I'm creating. It can't be helped, though. This is no time for a leisurely stroll or a cautious belly crawl.

An outcropping of seven or eight elephant-sized boulders juts up ahead of me. It makes a notable landmark and will more than likely allow me to see what lies ahead for at least a quasi-useful distance. From my steady jog, I push into a sudden sprint and cover the ground between myself and the big damn rocks in a couple of minutes. Not stopping, I use my momentum and strength to plant a rubber tread against the side of the first boulder and propel myself up a good ten feet to the top of the next.

Feet planted solidly, I land and immediately freeze my forward motion. Shit! I almost threw myself straight into the middle of a small group of my prey. Biting hard on my lip, I slowly lower myself against the warm and dusty gray rock in a pathetic attempt to blend in and make myself less of a visual target. The dense metal of my helmet adequately muffles my light pants, but it also stifles my breathing with its encapsulated design. Discomfort pushed aside, the helm remains in place. It provides my person with the extra layer of protection I need now.

A quick scan shows only nine Zee meandering below. Their body heat signals must have been blocked by my chosen perch and are now reading loud and clear. This is too small a group for those tracks, though. Most cells measure between 40-80 bodies. Where's the rest of the cell?

I risk a quick pop-up, sizing up the area immediately around me with my helm's scanners to try to identify any more of the target. Such a brief assessment doesn't register any additional Zee, but I don't find that reassuring. What to do? This small piece of the horde should be easy enough to dispose of, but I can't just unload my rifle. I risk alerting the absent primary group of my presence and, subsequently, my team's. No, it's better to play on the side of caution and go about removing the threat manually. This situation is precisely why Zeta soldiers are required to select a secondary weapon to specialize in that requires no ammunition and stores neatly on their person.

Securing my rifle in its resting position between my shoulder blades, I pull free the batons strapped along the outside of each of my thighs. Each bar is t-shaped and slightly longer than my forearm. The ones allocated initially to us in the service were composed of hickory wood or aluminum if you went for the collapsible kind. I lucked out with a hand-me-down from a more seasoned Zeta soldier that I bested in sparring. He was so impressed with my strength that he offered me his set of batons made from rare Australian ironwood. Please don't ask me for specifics, as I'm not an expert on wood and Janka hardness, or whatever. I know they're heavy as fuck and equally solid.

My strength lies in...well...my physical strength. The weapon I chose for close combat allows me to use my particular Zeta ability to its fullest and beat the ever-loving heck out of the enemy. Face grim and body tense, I center my mind in that calm place within before twisting out of my hidey-hole. I need to be noiseless about this. I can't allow these creeps to call out to their brethren.

The rasp of a fleshy shoulder sliding against the base of the boulder resounds obtrusively behind me. Gritting my teeth, I prepare to approach my prey from the opposite side and get the drop on it, only to practically run my faceplate into the snarling visage of a Zee. Backpedaling, I almost fall flat on my not-so-padded ass in my haste to get away. That was entirely stupid of me to fall for the classic trope of every horror flick I ever avoided as a child. Can't prevent living this real-life freak show, though. Within the HUD-lit interior of my helmet, my eyes narrow as cortisol floods my system, heightening my already stressed senses. That's it. Time to put these monsters down.

The first Zee doesn't even manage to turn before one weighted end crashes through its temple, fracturing its brittle jaw. The creature slumps over, making room for the next two. As I drop down and brace my left hand against the jagged rock-strewn ground, my right stows the baton and grabs the hilt of my combat knife. The K Bar slides silently and slickly from its holder along my calf—a firm and solid weight in my hand.

Sharp edges dig into the palm of my glove but don't manage to pierce the hardened leather. The thick muscles in my shoulder coil in preparation for a quick thrust into the second creature's throat. Hot blood spills over my hand, where I push the serrated edge of my weapon through tissue, muscle, and fat. I waste no time cleaning off the blade or myself as I turn and lunge out of my half-crouch to catch the next Zee right in the gut. The thing doesn't know it's dead yet. It releases a gurgling moan as it attempts to grab me, despite being disemboweled. That's the problem with these malignant beings. So long as electrical energy conducts throughout their bodies (or what remains of them), they keep coming.

I learned that particular fact during my basic training. When you're a green soldier pitted against actual Zee and testing your knowledge, skill, and survival instinct, you learn your enemy quickly. The alternative is that you get carried out in a body bag. It's brutal and borderline inhumane, but this isn't a harmless training exercise. It's the continued existence of what remains of humanity, and there's probably less than 5% of us non-Zee left. At least in the former United States. I have no clue how the rest of the world has fared. Globalism and Zee don't go together.

My knife lodges deeply into the temple of the Zee, clambering over the fallen mounds of its comrades. It collapses, joining the now-growing pile. Four down, five more to go. I have to employ a 'gymnastics move' to get at the remaining Zee. Using the piled and put-down Zee as an impromptu pommel horse, I use my hands to propel my body over them, swinging both legs hard into the torso of the nearest body. Both me and it go flying, but it at least outpaces me. With both batons in hand again, I put every ounce of my inhuman strength into bludgeoning the three left in a convenient semi-circle around me. Each strike and subsequent connection jars my shoulder and the joints in my arms. I push that sensation to the back of my mind as I lay waste to the Zee with a single-mindedness I typically suppress.

The blood rushing in my ears slows as I finally settle into a relaxed stance. The world around me seems to be blanketed in silence. Once I finally return to myself and take stock of things, I recall the last Zee I knocked away from the main group. Without looking far, I find the emaciated thing still on the ground, not moving. The force of my double kick must have ruptured something vital inside it. Good. Taking a brief respite to get my breath back, I chance a glance around, ensuring that I'm still in the clear and there's no other threat to be had.

WRONG PATH TAKEN

No way could that have been the primary cell I found signs of earlier. It's far too few to have left that much of a trail. This group probably veered off during their mindless march toward their next unsuspecting meal.

The tracks are scattered, as expected of Zee on the move. Okay, this is a problem. What did I miss? Looking for more clues will take time, but I can at least figure out where these Zee originated from. As usual, the horde has left a muddled mess of prints on the ground. It's a mix of bare feet, well-worn shoe treads, and the obvious drag marks of something that doesn't entirely fall into either the shoe or whole foot categories.

Wait. A few steps back, I notice that a good portion of the Zee's trail seems to go wide before doubling back the way they originated. It's just beyond where I had a run-in with the smaller fringe group. I come to an abrupt stop. What started as fifty or so unique sets of footprints is quite a bit more. Like, realistically, in the hundred-plus bodies range. No matter how good I am (and that's not a brag, it's a proven truth), I'm not that good. Any soldier with some semblance of common sense, whether Zee or human, knows better than to go against an enemy that seriously outnumbers them. I may be one badass Zeta soldier, but anything over fifteen to twenty solo pushes it for me. I don't want to be a dead fool.

Sudden, sick dread floods my stomach. The rest of the horde is heading in the direction of the camp. Well, this blows. Adrenaline floods my body as I sprint back to where my bike is waiting. Heart pounding forcefully in my chest, I think about Omicron and his gear. I calculate how far the team can have gotten in packing up between my original contact time and now. Shit. I don't come up with a good result. There's no point dwelling on the what-ifs now.

I skip through standard boot-up protocols with my ATC to get my ass out of there as quickly as possible. The ride back takes a lot less time than the initial trip out. I attempt to control my breathing and stay clear in my head. I'm still too far out in the field for my short-range Comms to work. I'll have to wait until I'm closer to pick up my team's open feed. Looking at the terrain map in my HUD, I can see the two dots representing my position and base camp getting closer together. Scenery streams by my visor in a blur as I push my bike to its limits attempting to get back to the team as quickly as possible. My thoughts keep looping around how I shouldn't have missed this. If I hadn't been so fixated on my earlier set-to, first with Omicron and then with Tau, perhaps my head would have been more in the game. As it is, I've wasted precious time fighting a small group while a much larger one could be overtaking my team. I should be there. I can feel it rumbling in my innards.

When I'm about 30 miles out, I finally pick up the crackle of static from an active line.

"Rho, are you there? Answer me, dammit."

More snaps and pops from feedback meet my hail. I nibble on my lip as I wait. It's a nervous gesture from grade school that I should have dropped years ago.

Rho's voice floods the line, and I all but sag in my saddle in relief.

"Yeah, Omega, we're here. What's up?"

"Rho, there's incoming. Have you made contact yet?"

He seems confused when he answers. "What incoming, Omega? We haven't seen one scrawny body, other than Chi's, anywhere. We're just about done packing up. Omicron's taking his sweet time, but I guess that's to be expected with that delicate flower of his."

"Crud. Okay, Rho. Everybody needs to be on high alert. There's a large-scale horde coming right at you. The ones I just encountered moved fairly quickly and had decent reaction time, so let's assume they're not as well-aged as we'd prefer. You need to be prepared for engagement."

"Get your ass back here. We'll be ready for them, Megs. How far out are you?"

"Looks like I have twenty clicks left. If I break the sound barrier slightly, I should be there in fifteen."

Rho chuckles. "Yeah, try not to crack up your bike before you get here. That won't do us much good."

My lower lip juts slightly despite my strict rule not to pout.

"Yeah, no, Rho. I'm not going to get into a frickin' accident on my way to save your sad and sorry asses. Thank you very much."

He chuckles. "Of course, Omega. We'll see you shortly then. Base out."

It can't be more than ten minutes later that I see camp on the horizon. It's pretty easy to identify where my scout and gunner are perched with what remains of our temporary luxury villas in my helm's sight. At least they're positioned as good little soldiers in an optimum spot for engagement.

I haven't even begun to slow in relief when I hear the first sharp report of gunfire. A few seconds after the initial shot, many, many more follow. I can tell it's mostly coming from the western side of camp, so the fighting appears to be away from the medic's tent—at least for the time being. On the downside, it's where our sleeping quarters are located.

Hopefully, my team was on it and is close to packed up and ready to go. It sucks to try to load gear with Zee breathing down your neck. I may have experienced it once or twice in the distant past, you know?

As I reach clear visual range, I see Rho and Chi taking shots one after another at the approaching undead. Each bullet is fired with the intent to kill. A head or throat shot that entirely debilitates and destroys. A few miss their mark because of an unplanned stumble or slump and glance off a shoulder or other nonessential part. The rule is that if you can't kill a Zee outright, you need to disable its method of locomotion. If you can't do that, you'd better be ready for hand-to-hand combat or to run.

LAST MAN ON THE GROUND

Between the hairs framing my face that are matted flat from sweat and the moist, stale air in my helmet, I'm doing my best not to dwell on my overall discomfort. This moment is in no way a good time for me to have a heat stroke. While very efficient at keeping the Zee out, our gear is like a lead weight hanging off my shoulders. Between the layers of body armor, under mesh, and an additional hard shell, I have 30 pounds of added weight to tote around without weaponry. Not that I deny its ability to save my ass, as it has done time and time again.

Taking in the battlefield, I pick out Chi's and Rho's taller forms. They're holding their own for now, with each focused on the Zee ahead and each other's sixes. Omicron and Mu seem most in need of my help, as the largest concentration of the horde appears to be focused on their position. Mu's selected the highest point possible in the area. Her position just so happens to be standing atop the back of her bike. Helmet off and pixie cut hair tugged by the light breeze, she's efficiently and calmly moving in a circle taking out any Zee coming towards her and Omicron's position. Her headshots fly without a hitch, one right after another. Thankfully, out of everyone's rounds, she has the most left. Last time we checked, at least. It's coming in handy now.

I can see that Omicron is trying desperately not to lose his shit. His larger form hastily works to get the remains of the medical supplies stored for transport. It seems like he was halfway through packing when all of this went down. The medic's patient is stretched out on a litter by Omicron's cycle. I doubt if the Alpha is even aware of what is happening around him. The medic readministered some heavy meds after my abrupt exit from his tent. The plan is likely for the patient to be loaded behind the big man's bike the moment Om gets enough of a breather to get out of here. That doesn't look like it will happen anytime soon, though.

I tap my de facto second on the shoulder to gain his attention.

"Rho, I'm going to help Omicron and Mu keep things tight in their quadrant."

The gunner spares a quick nod as he's entirely focused on the task at hand. Chi doesn't twitch when I cut a path behind her now crouched form. I put my all into getting to the rest of my people. Resolve firmly in place, I push my way toward where they are defending a potentially indefensible position. As I go, I dodge clusters of Zee trying to encroach upon our sides.

Guns in such a tight space aren't working too well. Instead, I stow my rifle and use my batons again. I might as well take the opportunity to remove anything that crosses my path thoroughly. As I said before, brute strength—mine enhanced far more than other Zeta soldiers— is where my power lies, and there's no way I'm not going to use it at this point.

The first Zee to meet my might loses the lower part of its face and drops to the ground, still grumbling, but hopefully not for much longer. The next few follow suit. Thus begins a rhythm of the enemy engaging me before I clobber them into paste.

One tries particularly hard to deter me from my self-appointed mission, trying to take a bite out of my left hand. I'm quick to smack it away with my mostly unoccupied dominant hand. The solid core of the baton makes a satisfying thud against its twisted face. That might have sickened me in the past, but it's music to my ears right now. Pushing the destroyed creature away, I dodge past the next set of grasping arms and hands, driving forward the last few yards to where my teammates are set up.

By the time I'm to the medic and sniper, their overall setup is tense. My original guess for the size of this horde was grossly underestimated.

There must be close to two hundred of these monsters closing in on us, and we've managed to clear only half of them. We're not in a position to cleanly remove them from our camp. Nor does it seem a good idea to try remaining here, as we're essentially cornered. I briefly consider Chi's incendiary rounds before sadly recalling that she used the remainder of them to get our resident Alpha out of the frying pan earlier this week.

I won't lie to myself—this is pretty dire, but there's no way I'll lay down my arms and let these creatures get the better of my team.

"Omicron, what can I help with?" My eyes and HUD continually scan for threats as I slide to a halt beside him.

He's not at all surprised by my sudden presence. The medic looks relieved to see me. Our last altercation is forgotten for now, but I'm betting it isn't entirely forgiven. He's also switched away from his primary weapon to what I have only ever been able to describe as a battle axe. I'm no stranger to Omicron's choice of a secondary, hand-to-hand combat weapon. It's pretty effective in this kind of situation.

Offhandedly, I notice that Omicron doesn't have his helmet on yet. A continuous layer of sweat is dripping down the broad planes of his face even though it's still early enough in the day that the heat hasn't set in. From her position above, Mu doesn't acknowledge me, but that's what I prefer. I'm more comforted by her having my back now than engaging in social niceties.

"Omega," Omicron gasps with whatever breath he has, "Help me grab the last of my monitoring supplies. I need to get them loaded, and we'll be good to go. I can do without the rest."

I look dubiously at the leftover piles but trust that Om knows better. I nod and drop my batons back into their holsters. If I can at least get Omicron and his charge out of here intact, I haven't failed.

Leaning down, I pick up one of the remaining heavy steel crates. It more than likely contains the UF's slightly outdated yet well-made medical equipment. I have to say that as much as I'd love the latest and greatest tech, this stuff works. Couple that with it outlasting anything else out here at the end of the world, and it's a win. Equipment that has been through real-life usage by the military over many decades can't be beaten, and I'll take one of these any day of the week.

I imagine it's been troublesome moving them alone, even for Omicron. Now, he may not have my kind of strength, but for a normally enhanced Zeta soldier, Om manages. For me, they require a little extra effort, but not too much. It's more of the awkwardness of not having long enough arms and bigger hands. Those would come in handy when grabbing this damn gear.

Loading the rest of our medic's kibble progresses smoothly enough, and I'm starting to feel a little twinge of that elusive thing called hope. But then I'm reminded that hope doesn't exist. I'm almost clipped by a bullet that whizzes by my faceplate. Mu's bound and determined to clear out all of the Zee. Best not to get in her way.

Now I feel increased pressure to get out of here, and I use some hidden reserve within to move even faster at stowing the rest of the supplies. On my peripheral, the HUD registers Omicron's proximity as he rushes to do the same.

I'm just closing the last clasp on his bike's tow-behind trailer when my display lights up red, and a pair of strong arms grab me around my waist, roughly pulling me down to the ground. I think it's our medic hauling me out of harm's way, but then I can feel the twitchy gestures and protruding bones pushing into the back of my shoulder blade. Disgusted, I elbow the damn thing in the rib cage. Not that it's a particularly effective self-defense move for these creatures; more just a reaction out of ingrained habit.

The Zee don't acknowledge their pain. They can't. I've seen a Zee running around halfway burned through, still on fire, and not faltering in its staggering steps as it pursues a meal. Scientists have yet to ascertain whether Zee can distinguish between physical pain and a lack thereof. Thankfully, no one has been dumb enough yet to check for emotional and psychological pain with our enemy. That would earn that particular individual a quick headshot from me.

With a swift gesture, I snap the forearm tightly grasped around my middle. My gut instinct is to throw the damn corpse as far away from me as possible. The creature snarls, and I use the opportunity to insert a quality body throw. It sails beautifully over my shoulder and into a couple of its advancing cohorts. That seems to do the trick for a second, but almost immediately, another one is trying again for me. Pushing the frothing once-man back enough to generate space, I unload my seldom-used 9mm into its face. Kicking the corpse away, I glance toward Omicron's position.

Oh, fuck me.

He's almost overrun as well. Even doing our best to pick them off, there are too many. This is not going to work. I hear Chi shouting something over Comms, but I can't decipher exactly what. I'm a little preoccupied with trying to keep from being torn apart, so hopefully, she'll forgive me for the lapse.

A face with rotted teeth and no doubt equally terrible breath looms. I have a brief moment of wondering if this might be the end when a shot rings out. The closest Zee's skull shatters right onto my thankfully closed faceplate. As the headless body falls over, I get ready to push through and hopefully make some headway. Another bullet whizzes by splintering its intended target into bony fragments. Subsequent shots now ring out, systematically taking out the next Zee, and another, and another.

"Wow, Mu's really on it today." However, I don't waste any time or effort in congratulating her.

I focus on the remaining Zee as the space around us opens. Chi and Rho seem close to being in the clear—enough, so they're heading our way. Things are getting reined under control. The team takes care of the last few fiends efficiently as I add a meager five or six to the final body count.

Mu sidles up along my right, not coming from where I expected her to be given that last volley. An odd confusion settles in as I put two and two together. I can only stare at our resident invalid lying in his makeshift cot at the other end of the transaction, rifle still raised unerringly in place. Sitting up in his litter, he looks half-dead but is no less firmly grasping his weapon with deadly intent shining in his eyes. With a quick nod to me, which I return half-consciously, he returns to picking off the remaining Zee to which he has a line of sight.

Returning to the fray, I finish clearing my area on autopilot. There may be more to this guy than I originally anticipated. His shots are immaculate. There's no hesitation or faltering. If I didn't know any better, that is the look of a man who wants to live.

ACT 4 - ANY DAMSEL IN A STORM

HIS OWN TWO FEET

After the slightly dramatic exit from our last camp, a good 200-mile ride brought us to the northern tip of what was called Nevada. We holed up in a primarily intact office building right smack dab next to nothing. Given that the next part of our journey will be mountains and buttes, Omicron pulled medical authority and deemed an empty, three-story office complex our rest and recovery spot.

Being able to sleep relatively safely (second-story living, though watch those derelict floorboards!), easy game hunting, and even the occasional sponge baths have made us as fresh and green as a new batch of Zeta soldiers. Even our charge has almost completely recovered, and none too soon. The dude is getting on everyone's nerves and irritating the hell out of me for more than one reason. Seriously. I've even seen the ever-jovial Mu actively avoiding his dour personage.

I'd chosen the western outer wall of said building to have a little quiet time within its tall shadows. Command wasn't the most thrilled at the last check-in. It took all of the self-restraint I could feebly grasp not to snap off to them. If there's any single individual to be held accountable for missed timelines, it's Tau for dropping an extra person and mission on us. One benefit of being a remote team is that the UF may huff and puff, but they can't do shit against us until we're back at base. That they're more than aware of this fact probably doesn't help their overall disposition with my team.

Regardless, they want that mysterious Alpha soldier returned as promptly as our collective superhuman asses can move. Allotting for charge time for our bikes in between drives, we're looking at a good couple of months at best until we breach Montana's southern border. Only then will we be able to drop the Alpha's ass at their mountainous doorstep. Inevitably, it will take longer, considering our primary missions are still active and a 'Complete' is not conditional.

157

"How long do we have to keep putting up with this guy?"

That drawn-out, nasally whine does nothing for my state of mind. I was already carrying around a bad mood the past few days. There's no need to add gunner-triggered irritation on top of that. Eyeballing Rho's goateed face where he bellyaches and fusses, I contemplate the most effective way to silence him. He's playing the part of a petulant, spoiled brat of a child to a tee.

Aggravation aside, I half-consciously appraise Rho's current condition as I habitually do when in the presence of any member of my team. As he stands there, tall and stance relaxed, his general state suggests a certain clarity and calmness attributable to getting consistent rest. For the last couple of weeks, we've been twiddling our collective thumbs to satisfy Omicron's insistence on having the Alpha at 100% physical health before we move on. Unsurprisingly, it's done everyone some good. Maybe even myself, so long as I don't focus on the two mission deadlines we've had to modify to adjust for the illustrious Tau's growing list of needs.

With a sigh, I drop out of my internal musings and address my now extremely impatient gunner. I grace him with a broad and sparkly grin, and the source of my morning ire takes a few hesitant steps away from my seated position. Not to be deterred by his lack of enthusiasm, I continue in what can only be dubbed my 'super happy mode.'

"Rho! How are you faring today? Are you finding your accommodations and dining options acceptable?" Not allowing him a word in edgewise, I continue my nice teammate act, talking over any started excuses. "That's good because I'd hate to see you... suffer unnecessarily."

He gulps at the dark look that I have now imposed upon him. Idiot. I snort at the thought. I glance toward where the root of our conversation sits, fixedly cleaning his disassembled rifle with all of the focus of an individual marked by OCD. Without a doubt, I know that his UF-issued weapon is in damn-near-perfect working order. I saw to its cleaning a week ago, and we've seen no action since even before then.

Physically, the soldier is doing well. It's a testament to Omicron's skill as a medic that he was able to bring the Alpha back from the brink of death in less than a fortnight. And with his patient clawing and screaming at him the whole time, no less. So far, my opinion about our sixth wheel is quite dismal and paradoxically as high as it's ever been about Om. I'm sure his patient could be a valuable asset to my team. The flawless shots he took as an invalid when we were almost overrun were admirable. Not that I said anything of it to him. In my defense, he passed out almost immediately afterward. Regardless, his aiding us would require the enormous effort of him pulling his head out of his ass. Seems unlikely at this point, even though he has a relatively small cranium.

Rubbing the worn fingertips of my gloves against each other, I consider our predicament. HQ ordered the Alpha delivered to them promptly and in no less than perfect condition. A tall order, to be sure. Mind you, we're supposed to accomplish this on top of our current six-month assignment. Currently, we're only a third of the way through our routinely scheduled missions. So, we now have an additional, overlapping duty that will require resources and time at present not available to us. Considering both sets of orders came from the same issuing office, you would think they would have noticed the conflict. Can I be the only one who sees a problem with this setup?

Rho attempts to clear his throat and gain my attention quietly. Raising my eyes to his, I lift an eyebrow in question. I notice he's accrued some scruff around his wide mouth over the last couple of days. Apparently, he hasn't felt the need to be entirely up to regs.

"So..." he starts, shifting nonchalantly from one leg to the other. "What are we going to do now?"

Exhaling, I almost shrug my shoulders out of old habit but resist the urge. "Frankly, the only thing we can do is escort the princess back to the castle. We haven't the power or choice to do otherwise."

"And the rest of our assignment?"

"It will be completed according to schedule. No excuses." I hold a hand up to stall any adverse reactions. There's no gray area in the matter, so there's no point in explaining or arguing. "HQ expects the Alpha to support our team for the remainder of our orders. At least there's that small allowance." Leaning back against the cool steel, I pull my arms above my head and get in a good stretch, straightening both my shoulders and upper back. "We have an estimated four months to get from here to there. Oddly convenient, that is also what we have left of our present mission timeline."

The tall, auburn-haired gunner slumps forward, head hanging down and pouting again. I know how he feels. I'm just better about not projecting it to the world at large. More of the hide and suppress it type.

"In other words, this dude has hijacked us. Great. I guess I'd better start endearing myself to him."

"Why bother? He's not part of the team. We'll be rid of him in no time. Not worth investing energy into any attachments. He's also made it abundantly clear how much he does not love the situation or our role in it."

Rho looks at me kind of funny. Like I missed the punchline of some obvious joke.

"Well…" he clears his voice a bit. "You're interested in the intel that he's carrying, right? So, at least one of us should try being the 'good cop' part of the time."

I stiffen upon hearing those words, immediately cognisant of my error. I was so focused on the disruption that is Tau that I didn't bother planning two steps ahead to obtain my goal. Leave it to Rho to figure out the politics behind a situation. It's a surprise he hasn't made it further in the UF, given his natural tendency towards strategic thinking and human manipulation.

One of the best things to do as a leader is to recognize your strengths and weaknesses and who around you can be relied upon to complement them. I'll never make nice, nice with the Alpha. That's for damn sure. My gunner, however, is a master of coercion and persuasion.

"Go for it. I'm in full support of you ingratiating yourself."

"You're kidding, right?"

I snort at his doubt. "No joke. I attempted another conversation with his royal highness a few mornings ago, and the only thing he could be bothered to say was how much I suck at being a team leader. Something about scraping the barrel for me to be an option?"

Rho cackles with glee. "Aw, man. No way!" He relaxes in his stance, hands positioned on each hip and a lazy grin shaping his long face. "And I'm sure you were the picture of empathy and understanding, right?"

Scratching at a non-existent itch on my chin, I smirk and respond glibly, "Oh, yes. I gave him the care and consideration someone of his status deserves."

Shaking his head in amusement, Rho finally turns around and slides his scrawny rear down the wall to thump onto the ground next to me without any invitation. It may not seem possible, but there are times when things like rank and decorum mean something to my teammates. We've become very familiar with each through our five-plus years of nomadic isolation from the remains of society. It builds an inherent dependency on our teammates. Maintaining a typical unit's standard distance and propriety is challenging with the awful stuff we've experienced together. It drives into the individual soldier a profound sense of loyalty and kinship. It's hard to imagine not being with these idiots day in and day out.

Rummaging around in one of the many small pockets along the breast of my flak vest, I pull out a slender, faded blue tin. Rho perks up immediately. Popping the longer side open with my free thumb, I expose the neatly nested stack of cigarettes; all lined up and ready to go. Pinching the ends of a couple, I slide them free from their little elastic belt. One is rubbed, then popped between my slightly chapped lips, while the other is offered to my gunner. He eagerly grabs it, putting the filtering end to his mouth as I click the container closed and shove it back into its hidey spot.

There's no need to ask for a light as the redhead is already holding his out to me. The meager device is just as pathetic in size and stature as our smokes. The stubby metal cylinder is not longer than my pointer finger and about as thick. It almost dwarfs the pinky-sized cigarettes with their mostly filtered length. The end of civilization left behind one too many "it's good for you" things in its wake. For example, a cigarette sans the pleasure of a dopamine rush. I never paid attention to social policies and the like; however, it's incredible how much you notice those things when there's little to serve as a distraction.

The end lights up quickly as I take a slight drag in. Glowing orange embers dance merrily as they're enkindled into life. It's early enough that the air still has a crisp, new quality. For several minutes all there is to hear are the quiet puffs of Rho and me smoking our non-cigarettes and the chirping of whatever small birds have decided to claim our warehouse as their home. Or perhaps it's the opposite. After all, those squatty little balls of feathers hopping from perch to perch were here first. Their ignorance of the new world order around them puts our world into a rather dismal perspective.

I think there's some famous commentary about how animals and such will eventually inherit the world. Seems like humanity has made that an almost sure thing at this point. Now less than concerned, I hold my cig out in front of me, loosely balancing the tiny stub of what's left. In no time, its trail of gray smoke thins to a trickle before extinguishing itself on my fingertips.

With a deep sigh, I snuff the remainder into the dry earth beneath me, grinding it to nothing. Any remaining material will break down further, given a few days' exposure to the elements. One invention those 'green world' folks got right. I brush my rough palms against each other twice before planting them firmly on my thighs and pushing back up to a standing position.

Looking around the filtered haze, I can tell we're nearing mid-morning and close to shift change. That means border patrol for Rho and babysitting duty for me. Shrugging off my lack of enthusiasm at the thought, I tilt my head, eliciting a nice, sharp crack in response. I'd say that I'm getting too old for this, but I don't think that's a true statement anymore.

Catching Rho's eye from where he still sits, staring blankly into the distance, I gently clear my throat. He starts and blinks hard before turning his attention toward me.

"Shift change," I supply, grinning broadly. The gunner slumps in response before perking up. An evil glint comes to his eye, making me wary.

"Doesn't that mean you have Alpha duty?"

I grace him with a long-suffering look. "Yes. No need to bring that up. Bad enough having to tolerate his presence without being up close and personal."

"Didn't think he did personal." The flat look he receives from me isn't meant to be encouraging. "Aww, you'll be fine. Just lay some of that good old Omega-branded charm on him. He won't be able to resist."

The ass dares to give me one of his foxlike grins before hopping up to two feet. His 6-foot-plus stature easily dwarfs mine, and I can't help the automatic glare. I do hate being this height. What I wouldn't give to have received my size from the other half of my lineage. It would make putting dopes like Rho into his place a much simpler feat. Good thing I can always kick his ass.

I flick a quick hand to shoo him off. He chuckles at it but complies without further shenanigans. With a barely squashed whine, I turn and orient myself towards the latest rendition of a med bay and my hell. Hopefully, my charge will be unconscious or, at the very least non-communicative. I prefer that over him running his mouth.

FULL OF SOMETHING

The walk to Omicron land takes far less time than I would prefer. There are better ways to spend my morning than interacting with Tau. I'm not the only one of that opinion, excluding Om. He tends to become neutral with most patients when they are under his care. That is, except for Rho. Unsurprising from my perspective.

Too deep within my mind, I fail to notice when my feet bring me almost directly into another pair of UF-issued boots. Off-handedly I notice that they look close to the same size as mine. I don't startle outright, but I'm sure my face betrays me as I feel it heat slightly. I had no idea the medic had unleashed his medical pet.

The Alpha soldier stands unmoving in my path, his glare firmly affixed at my person. In my defense, I have not had a real conversation with the guy since what I think of as 'the med bay incident.' Eyes flicking briefly over his form, I note the lack of bandages and blood stains. Probably a good sign of his health and recovery. Yay.

"Tau." I intone, both in greeting and question.

His cheek twitches minutely in response, but that's all the reaction that I garner from him. The soldier is partially outfitted at present. His traditional clothing, vest, and gauntlets are in place—Alpha gold colored, of course—but he's without a poncho or weaponry. My eyebrows rise at that last fact.

Attempting again to be civil and not state something inane about the weather, I continue as if this is an actual exchange. "Have you been released from medical by Omicron?"

Arms crossed and chin tipping up ever-so-slightly, Tau confirms. "Yes, I have been cleared by your medic for duty."

His voice is quieter than I remember. Pitched lowly enough to require additional focus to catch what he's saying. Not at all like the well-projected voices command staff tend to develop, partially from loud artillery but also from trying to get morons to listen. That seems like an intentional behavior on Tau's part. Putting the ownness on the listener to figure out what you're mumbling, then probably correct them when they get the message wrong.

"Good. Then you can get on the roster and take up some of the assignments around camp. I assume you're okayed for lifting and actual physical work, right?"

His lip curls up, giving me the impression that he doesn't like me all that much, regardless of my tone. Too bad for him. This is my team.

"I am not some recruit you can assign to whatever labor you wish, Omega."

"Oh, so you do remember my name." I lean into his personal space, grinning. "Well, you should also remember that I am the Commander of this Zeta squad, and you are under my authority. You will address me accordingly."

His face flares red as I shift back a little, and I await the fallout with maybe a little too much relish.

"If you are such a fine leader, answer me this—where is the sixth member of your team?"

The sound of flesh and bone connecting solidly with more of the same substance resounds loudly in the silence left in the wake of that statement. Belatedly, I blink, and the world around me slowly swims back from its watery state into a grainy focus. My right hand is tingling—particularly at the knuckles. A lithe body draped in taupe garb is laid out at my feet.

Thankfully, it's just Tau.

His lax form does not twitch as I relax and straighten from my coiled stance. Consciously, I have to force my right hand to unclench and form something other than a fist of death. The sound of sand crunching under multiple incoming hurried steps breaks the ringing in my ears. I observe with a certain disconnected apathy as Omicron brushes forcefully by me and crouches next to the Alpha's splayed body. As the medic checks my victim over, no sound is made by the remaining team members who have joined us.

I imagine that they are holding their collective breath at Omicron's diagnosis. After a minute and a half of doing God knows what, the dark-skinned man leans back on his heels.

Flashing a tired look and a thumbs up to the rest of the camp, he states, "He'll live, folks. It looks like the Commander dialed it back."

Fixing a glower at the unconscious form, I'm hard-pressed not to kick a stray akimbo limb for good measure. Damn. It really would be my luck that I barely throw a punch when my usual strength would have solved more than one problem. It is a shame that I didn't 'accidentally' break his neck. Well, many treacherous things are lying between us and our destination. For Tau to succumb to some mishap would be easy to explain away in our line of work. They don't even demand the body as proof anymore—it is too inconvenient for the UF to deal with a Zeta soldier's remains humanely.

This Alpha continues to be an ongoing issue for me, beginning when we accepted that thrice-damned mission to rescue his team. Had I known what that mission and that day would have brought, I might have gone AWOL with my team and saved myself the trouble of a court-martial later on when I finally ended up taking care of this asshole permanently. Little did I know that we would get saddled with the miserable leftovers of a massacred Zeta team for our foreseeable future.

I disinterestedly pick out a few granules of dirt beneath my middle digit fingernail as Omicron binds a cooling pack to the prick's jaw. Once he's done, the medic hefts our resident Alpha's still underweight form, carrying him bridal style to the medical tent as Mu follows closely, no doubt to help him care for the unconscious form inside.

Huh. What a waste of energy.

Once the excellent doc is satisfied with how his latest patient is set up, he returns to our still-assembled grouping. A good-natured pat on the sniper's shoulder has her running back to whatever she had occupied herself with before the fiasco. I catch her humming an old-time peppy little pop tune as she passes me without a look. Turning back to where she came from, Omicron gives me an unreadable expression at first before simply sighing and shaking his head.

"He'll be just fine, Commander. I imagine it will be a few hours before his jaw lets him speak properly and another few days before he says anything."

Nodding sharply once, I turn my back to the medic's knowing smirk and head off in the opposite direction. A short walk and some time to shoot at random things should help me clear up any lingering thoughts or voices regarding the matter. Time to let out my inner redneck.

When my Comms flare up, I've only managed to rid our present domain of a small number of the vermin, reptiles, and birds that share this location.

"Omega, contact!" My second's voice crackles loudly over the open line. Instinctively I turn to the last direction I saw Rho heading towards, ready to school him on using the team Comm for his hysterics. He's no newbie fresh out of Basic. The idiot should know better than to emote into the mic. At the same time, I scout for a clue as to what he's seen, doing my best to follow his line of sight.

Finally, I spot the anomaly. There's someone or something out there, but it's not a Zee horde. Nothing that exciting. The shape is wrong, and the movements don't match what we've become overly familiar with. Jogging lightly to where Rho stands with his rifle held at the ready, I fix my gaze on the same point beyond camp. The sun is currently in the worst position it could be, blinding us to the details of our trespassers. This approach could be intentional on the part of an enemy or simply perchance. Regardless, my hackles are up, and I'm on high alert.

Blinking through forced tears, I finally make out what appears to be a couple of figures walking, albeit slowly, alongside a… wagon? No way.

I'm struck dumb gazing at what appears to be an actual, Old West-style wagon, complete with a pair of yoked oxen pulling it. Did we break through space and time? Scientists were close to figuring out that whole 'time travel' thing. You know? When they weren't screwing with human genetics and dooming the world to being overrun by the horde. Having basically everyone turned Zee probably stopped that notion from ever reaching fruition during this round of human civilization.

"What's your count, Rho?" I call to him.

Without looking my way, he shouts back, "At least three of them— two are on foot, and there must be a third driving. They're moving steadily but too slowly to tell how they're armed."

Nodding, I push the small orange button inset into my throat piece. "Team, do you read me?"

There's a brief crackle of static followed by silence on the line. Then I hear Omicron.

"Yeah. We're here, Omega. What's up?"

"It looks like we have a small group of persons moving north of us. They're going slowly. As of now, Rho and I cannot determine their threat level."

"Roger that. How would you like us to proceed?"

Glancing towards the interlopers, I consider our options. We can choose not to engage them first but risk being surprised later. They're not too far off, but they are not necessarily heading toward our position. Right then. Decision made.

"Okay. Rho, you're with me. Let's take this slow and by the book. Mu, I need you to take Rho's position and watch our six. The rest of you—keep things tight and be prepared to provide backup if needed. They seem to be carting something, so there's a chance they have some kind of artillery. Got it?"

A chorus of affirmatives rings in my ear. Brushing by my second, I remove the safety from my rifle, weapon at the ready, and all senses open. As Rho and I casually stroll toward a potential enemy, the world around us sharpens, and I'm prepared to strike. There's no telling what we'll encounter.

AN ESCORT EXTRAORDINAIRE

As we close the distance between us and the target, my senses are thrown wide, taking in our surroundings. I can count on Rho being watchful as well. There's no scent of decay on the light morning breeze—the air is crisp and fresh. The birds, insects, and other small fauna moving about the desert floor ignore us and go about their daily lives. Whoever we're approaching, more than likely, they're not Zee. However, just because they're someone other than a voracious predator doesn't necessarily indicate they're good humans.

We've encountered many individuals out here who are less than congenial to the United Forces and its soldiers during our time out here. Unsurprisingly, the best of humanity isn't who survived this shit storm. Some of the more loathsome members of society outlived some more deserving folk. The difficulty lies in what to do with the 'bad guys.' The UF doesn't specifically outlaw firing on non-Zee combatants. However, the last thing we need to do is to evoke fear or distrust of the UF. Avoiding conflict is our primary directive with unaffected humans.

Ah, me. What to do when one option ends in a court-martial, and the alternative is a bullet to your skull? You have your ass ready for either scenario and the confidence that your decision is correct. Now isn't the time to noodle things over, as we're almost to their position.

I begin to hear voices by this point of the breathy, feminine variety. With a mournful glance at my companion, I silently pray to whatever god is receptive that attractive women aren't afoot. It's sadly a regular pattern of my de facto second to get sidetracked by anything lacking a Y chromosome. We both need to control the situation, or things can become much more dangerous. A Zeta soldier must always be ready to react at a moment's notice. No mercy is allowed. We need to take that headshot before they can.

With my pulse elevated, I slow our approach when we're about 10 feet away from the wagon's side. The contraption has stopped entirely and the two hefty animals pulling it seem unconcerned with our presence, lazily munching on whatever passes for grass around their cloven feet. From here, I attempt to gauge our potential enemy better. The wagon does remind me of something straight off the Oregon Trail. I can only guess its origin. Perhaps a relic kept in shape as a tourist attraction on a random, Old MacDonald farm. It may have been acquired from a studio's props department in the massive crater once known as Hollywood.

The string of material strung haphazardly along its sides like some random party decor is a bit more modern in design. As a the light breeze travels along the wagon's exterior, the strips of cloth flash, blindingly reflecting the sun's light. The fabric pieces initially caught my eye when I sighted the anomaly earlier. I couldn't recognize what it was from that distance, but in a way, I'm glad that I couldn't. This thing is just plain gaudy.

Regardless of the poor taste in accents, the wagon is functioning and doesn't appear to be carrying artillery. The ruts from its wheels in the soft-packed ground are too shallow to be hauling that kind of weight. That's a good sign in my book, but I will remain unconvinced and suspicious until I can confirm a lack of threat.

The figures from earlier are noticeably absent, as are any signs of activity. Rho and I glance at each other through our helmets before quickly returning our attention to the covered rear area of the wagon as a head of chestnut hair pops out, then just as quickly retreats.

What the hell? I feel like I've crossed into some alternate universe.

Watching the spot with misgivings, the same girl appears again and stays this time. Young and female. She's got to be sixteen... maybe eighteen, with tanned skin lighter than Omicron or Mu's but darker than mine, complete with long, brown braids and a dimpled smile. All of that is followed by a bouncy wave and a "Hello!" before she dodges back into the carriage.

Rho shifts as if to wave back, and I'm quick to throw a hard elbow into his open side. His helm turns towards me askance, but I'm well versed in ignoring him. He hastily flips his faceplate up in indignation, but I'm good at ignoring that. Without speaking to Rho, I turn and convey, through posture and body language alone, 'Not a word from you. Leave this to me.'

He huffs and gives me a dirty look before slapping his faceplate back into place and turning his head away. I get a warm fuzzy from nixing that particular line of stupidity. I don't give my second much thought after that.

The stopped wagon is wholly still, save for a few low voices and the sound of something or someone shifting. The two of us wait patiently, standing as comfortably and casually as two well-worn soldiers possibly can, particularly when facing an unknown situation.

A moment or two elapses before a pair of oversized combat boots slither their way over the lip of the wagon's open aft end. There's a brief moment of whoever's bottom hanging precariously in the air before they land gracelessly, more or less on their feet. It's the same girl from earlier, and thankfully she's so layered in drab, mismatched clothing items that they practically engulf her. Somehow, I still get the feeling that my gunner's eyes are bugging out.

Three additional forms follow the first girl's exit. They're each youngish, reasonably attractive women, but all dressed in that strange, mishmash clothing style as the original female. Not that I expect a lot of opportunity for high-end fashion in this day and age. My only saving grace is that the UF has plenty of taupe-colored uniforms in all of the different flavors of garment you could ever need.

We all stand there gauging each other. I, for one, am singularly unimpressed with our unexpected company. At first assessment, they might as well be straight out of the diverse Barbie four-pack. Each one's hair and skin tone are distinctly different, as are their expressions. My careful observation catches looks of suspicion, fear, anticipation, and even some underlying eagerness on their part. That last one throws me. I can't imagine we seem welcoming or approachable standing here in full gear with weapons at the ready.

Outwardly, they appear to be no significant threat. Perhaps they are lucky fools who have miraculously managed to remain alive through mere chance and timing. However, if I don't go with my opening assumption that these women are a bunch of simpering ninnies, it opens the door to other things. Like them intentionally appearing weak and non-threatening.

There's more going on here than what is readily apparent, of that I'm certain. And that is something to digest mentally. Unknowns leave me wary.

Tapping one of the preset buttons on my helm, I hail Rho, and only Rho, over communications. Our helmets are designed to block outside sounds and keep personal interactions private from external parties. This feature is handy for both the semi-coherent humans and the non-comprehending Zee listening for easily accessible prey.

"Hey, Rho. Don't drop your guard. These girls couldn't have survived this long without weapons or aid. We're not privy to something—I wish I knew what."

"Yeah. You're not going to believe it, but I was thinking along the same lines, Megs. Too convenient?"

"Yup. You didn't happen to pick up on any unusual discrepancies in your scans?"

"Nope! Zilch, as far as I've seen. They're squeaky clean."

"That makes two of us. Damn."

They're not a visible threat, but I'm loathe to let them out of our sight. Looking at their little isolated group of openness, I hear a voice suspiciously like Mu's discerning tone imploring me to, at the minimum, extend common courtesy to them.

With regret, I inform Rho of my decision. "Let's hear them out and see if we can decipher what is happening. They may have intel on this area that we can benefit from."

No sooner have I spoken than Rho's unbuckling his helm. With a flourished sweep and pull to the side, the dull metal covering is pulled off and tucked neatly under an arm, revealing my second's grinning visage. Megawatt smile firmly in place, Rho has magically slicked back his typically spiky, auburn hair away from a long and narrow forehead. The prominent UF-issued rifle has just as quickly disappeared, completing his approachability.

"Hi, there! I'm Rho. It's lovely to come across such a nice group of folk out here. We hardly ever get to run into new people, particularly of the unaffected variety."

I resist the urge to smack my de facto second upside the head, as well as slap my forehead for good measure. The dude is embarrassing. Reluctantly, I follow his lead for once. As soon as I'm released from the claustrophobic feeling of being enclosed in my helm, I shake my head and take in some air. It's not that the filters don't work in our helmets or the metal chafes or pinches as older models did. Having your head and face surrounded by metal makes it stifling and uncomfortable. I've known recruits that couldn't become full soldiers because of phobias around our required headgear.

Eyes dissecting the group before me, I find myself drawn to who appears to be the eldest person in their group. Her jet-black hair is tightly bound in a single, long braid, complimenting olive skin and a serene half-smile. She has an air of maturity, even though she's unlikely to be much older than me. Regardless, I note the others giving her their attention through sidelong glances, more than likely for guidance. Based on these few micro-interactions I witnessed within their group, she's probably my best bet for getting some answers.

"You've entered a United Forces clearing zone. I am Omega, and this is Rho, my second in command. I'm in charge of this Zeta Squadron. What's your business here?"

There you go. Polite and concise. No fluff or pointless 'getting to know you' platitudes at this point. It's my comfort zone, frankly. Let's be straight. I'm not what you'd consider good-natured or empathetic by any means. Never have been and have never felt bereft of it. Product of my childhood, I imagine. I have zero desire to take on more charges if that's what they seek. We've just finished playing nursemaid to one invalid. I don't want to subtract one and add four.

The taller woman takes a slight step back. Perhaps in fear or uncertainty? A thin, delicate hand rises to her chest as she takes as step closer to the others. I guess my direct approach was unexpected. The young woman shifts, overlapping skirt rustling as the color drains from her cheeks, leaving her unusually pale-complexioned. This dip in character happens for a moment before she regains her earlier poise. There's a cleared throat before she responds, giving a modest curtsy.

Seriously?

"How do you do? My name is Morgan, and these are my companions. We're seeking a small encampment of survivors we have been told were in this vicinity not too long ago."

"An encampment?" I parrot her words back, incredulity creeping into my voice as I glance at Rho. He looks equally perplexed.

"We haven't run into anyone else in this sector," my partner begins confidently before his face screws up as he thinks aloud. "Well…I guess sort of, but he's one of ours. So, that's probably not what you were thinking, right?"

She appears to think about it before quietly responding to my second. "No, I don't believe so."

Eyeballing how Rho melts at the attention, I am hard-pressed not to beat his ass into the ground. Big mistake! He knows better than to disclose UF intel to civvies, however minor it may be. I'll have to reeducate him on it once we're back at camp and out of earshot of anyone else. I press on where he's left off, hoping to divert this conversation toward something more productive and less sensitive in context.

"I'd recommend that you search elsewhere. We've come across plenty of loose hordes of Zee roaming this sector. If there was a survivor enclave around here, they've probably moved on, else I doubt there'd be anything left of it. Or them."

My words and tone convey precisely what I think—that there are no other possibilities.

The women slump, turning to each other crestfallen at the news, but as I watch closely, I note the dry eyes and lack of what would be a more profound disappointment. The one with bright apple green eyes and mocha skin questions me, undeterred by either my tone or what are inarguably the facts of this world. I absently note the reddish-gold hue of her hair. Unusual but natural. No red irises in this group. All are unchanged.

"They're nomadic by nature and have managed to survive here for months. Not some stationary refugee camp. Isn't it possible that their movements may have escaped your notice?"

The one called 'Morgan' gives a small a-hem before the darker-skinned girl flushes mauve, face sullen as she avoids looking directly at me.

"My name's Kari, by the way."

"Kari then," I smirk at her embarrassment before brushing it aside, "This is a large space, and yes, of course, it's possible and even probable that our paths haven't crossed yet. However, there's also a high likelihood that one of the roaming Zee hordes would have caught up with them by now. Unless your group is well-trained and touting some weaponry, the odds are not in their favor. They're currently not in yours either."

I suppose my end statement is unnecessary, but I feel morally obligated to point out how dumb it is to retain hope at this juncture.

The tight-lipped look I'm given is difficult to read. Cocking my head to the side, I appraise the redhead. "Where did you say that you're from again?"

Her eyes widen before narrowing in irritation. I observe her response, attempting to gauge whether her reaction is from me or the question. Being secretive can stem from many reasons, several of which concern me.

Clearing her throat, she regains a semblance of control. "We all started from different places but have chosen to journey together. It's safer and more practical for all of us as our destination is the same."

I cannot detect any lies within what she stated, but omitting details is just another tool of deception. Easier to hide too. I opt to approach things differently as my current goal is to build rapport with this group. At this point, focusing on something less likely to get their hackles up is probably a safer bet than pushing further about their origins. Hopefully, there will be more time for it later when I can unleash some of the more convincing members of my team at them.

"How old is your info if you had to take a guess?"

The dark-skinned girl starts at the subject change but dutifully glances at the fourth and final member of their group.

"Two weeks?" she asks for confirmation.

The tall wisp of a woman has stick-straight blond bangs and a face so fair there's no possible way she's ever spent a day outside without being burnt.

Without hesitation, she concurs in a strong, low voice. "Two weeks."

A firm nod accompanies her statement, as does a more than passing glance at Rho. He notices the look, unsurprisingly, and I almost groan out loud at his attempt at a rakish grin thrown her way. She smiles fully, cheeks rosy with pleasure at his notice.

"I'm Janet, by the way." She tells my second, completely ignoring me in her declaration. Not that I give a rat's ass, but it gives Rho a more oversized head than the dude typically walks around with.

Taking in the well-risen sun, I consider our options. I don't feel like dealing with this today, but there's little choice. It's moot for me to argue over statistical realities. It's also counter-intuitive to my earlier point for us to stay out in the open when we can discuss the whys and wherefores of their presence in our relatively protected site. Based on what I've observed, I don't believe there's an immediate danger from these females. Even if they might pose a threat, I'm confident my team can handle them. Extending our camp to these women seems a calculated risk worth taking for us.

"Look. If you need a reprieve, you can join my team at our temporary quarters. It's not much—just an old office complex missing a side. But it's mostly sheltered from the elements and about as safe as you can get around here. I can't vouch for the quality of the food, though. We're mostly feasting on MREs."

Kari immediately turns to the girl we initially encountered, who I've figured is the youngest amongst the femmes by this point. "What do you think, Anne?"

With all of the exuberance of youth, the brunette quickly replies, "That sounds awesome! Can we?" Her head turns so quickly to ask their elder that her braid flicks out widely, almost catching the darker-skinned girl in the face. She deftly dodges the swing as if used to doing so regularly.

By this point, Janet has stopped making googly eyes at my gunner and appears to be awaiting the tall, dark-haired woman's decision. She regards them all, lingering on where Anne and Kari stand side-by-side. After a moment, her eyes blink closed as she nods to the younger, half smile gracing her face like an indulgent parent.

"Yes, I don't see why that doesn't seem reasonable. We could all use the break from our travels. And it would be lovely to spend some time with your people, Commander Omega."

And just like that, it's settled. There's a chorus of "Yays" as the older girl announces their collective decision. I notice that Rho's tenor is included in that chorus.

Their enthusiasm is somewhat nauseating, but that feeling in my chest indicates that at least this decision is along the right path.

Turning to my lanky sidekick, I issue a quick set of verbal instructions with recording names and origins from the band of refugees. I don't need to ask him to mentally catalog everything else that he sees. Rho has a knack for remembering details with a clarity that seems even better than seeing them at present with my own two eyes. I want to know if anything is missing from these girls.

There is the slightly dismal thought that leaving the gunner unsupervised with the fairer sex for any amount of time is asking for Bad Things to Happen. Given the risks I routinely take in this line of work, I'll let Rho's overactive libido fall on the lower end of my concerns.

I untuck my helmet from my side and place it over the mass of fluff that is my hair. I don't wait for the clasp to secure before I hail the other slice of my team.

"Yo, Omicron, over."

His low-key bass answers immediately. "Here, Omega. Go ahead."

"I need you to prepare for some unexpected civvies temporarily shacking up with us. Secure anything classified and move it out of the line of sight. You got it?"

As my agitation lessens, my heart rate and senses follow. There's nothing worse than being locked in a heightened state of awareness. I'm sure the inherent stress alone takes hours off my proverbial clock. Not that I think of my life as existing in the long term. No. Instead, I live by the day, the hour, and the minute. There's no guarantee that I will still exist a decade, let alone a year from now.

"Do you want me to make a sleeping space for them?"

Thinking about that, it's probably the best option. I'd prefer to have them within spitting distance, and controlling their placement is an excellent way to ensure that.

"Yes. The second floor has that open foyer with a solid floor, right? Plan for them to stay there. It should keep them safe from Zee stragglers and within our purview. It's a group of four younger women. They seem to be transient and unarmed at the moment."

I'm about to turn back to my gunner when I remember to add. "Oh, and they have two oxen as well."

There's a noticeable pause before Mu's voice breaks over the line. Curiosity colors her cheerful voice.

"Really?"

I can't help the chuckle that escapes me. "Yeah, really. These women have two bulls pulling a GD wagon decked out in shiny ribbons. No shit."

"Oh. Okay." She sounds just as perplexed as I feel. It's too surreal for my taste. "No worries. We'll be ready for you."

"Roger that. We'll be there in twenty to thirty minutes. Omega out."

Communication over with, I head to where Rho has finagled himself, right into the center of the gaggle of giggling girls.

Yeah, say that five times fast.

"All done?" I prompt impatiently.

He has the wherewithal to nod meekly, although the dude is beaming with joy. Almost glowing, really. Ugh. Fuck my life.

Once again, I remove the upper portion of the thrice-accursed helmet, absently wiping away a line of sweat that had made its way into the line of my eyebrows. Thankfully, I have my unibrow in place to delay its advance briefly. Have I mentioned that we're SOL for personal items out here? Tweezers are hard to come by and harder not to misplace.

Regarding all five individuals, I do a quick once-over of the wagon train and the females before continuing.

"Alright. You're welcome to stay with us and get some rest. My team will move on shortly, but we can share space and safety for now. There's enough clean tap water and local wildlife to sustain everyone for a bit."

Their elation is palatable. Like, gag me. Oh, dear God. What have I stepped in? I continue holding up a single, gloved finger to forestall any further joy.

"However, we answer to the United Forces, and our first and only priority is to them. We may leave without notice, so don't expect our presence. Also, all of you need to respect and keep a healthy distance from all UF property, including my soldiers. No relations or fraternization. Understood?"

Further tittering and blushing results from my layout of the ground rules. That is not reassuring. Thank whatever god above or demon below that all Zeta soldiers are sterile. I'm sure that Rho will probably be familiar with at least one of these girls before we move on from their company. Well, Rho and maybe Chi. Hell, she'd probably stand a better chance of scoring, given her personality versus Rho's.

The one who I've decided is their leader shushes the others with the patience of a tenured elementary school teacher. She waits for them to calm down before addressing me.

"Please forgive my sisters their manners. I don't think we are used to having things so plainly and bluntly explained."

Here she gives me a soft smile like some indulgent older sibling.

I fully expect another curtsy or a demure nod, but I am pleasantly surprised by an empty hand held palm up and outstretched. Such an oddly familiar gesture cuts through my internal monitor rather effectively, and I grasp her outstretched hand in my leather-encased one. The careful eyes that meet mine are almost blue-gray in hue. An eye color I have not seen for some time.

She cautiously takes in my expression, and I'm struck with the impression that she is not as carefree and soft as I assume. This woman knows well enough not to trust others entirely, even someone from the United Forces. Perhaps especially a UF soldier. With a firm nod that both confirms and agrees with our mutual appraisal, we release the other before taking a step back to better distance ourselves.

At this point, I notice that she's a good head taller than me. Maybe a head and shoulders, if I'm being honest with myself. Seriously? Am I the shortest adult woman left in the world? I do my best not to show irritation at such a trite and silly thing.

With a curt smile, I tilt my head towards the direction of our user-friendly and quite temporary home.

"Shall we?"

INTRIGUING GUESTS AND INTRIGUE

A soft breath of wind caresses my face upon my first step outside the office's low rise. I need the space after getting four odd strangers settled into our makeshift camp. My irritation is less concerned with the visitors and more with my team's reaction to them.

Rho's eagerness is anticipated, though not appreciated. Omicron and Chi are relatively neutral in that they accept the change but otherwise are unaffected by the presence of these women. Mu is surprisingly irritable and has become curt and abrupt with just about everyone. Tau. Ugh. Don't get me started. I should have figured he'd take issue with the civvies, but I am sure to get an earful from the Alpha soon. He simply has this expression on his face. As if he shoved too big a bite of sushi or something in his mouth but is holding back spitting it out for fear of mixed company. It would be amusing if I wasn't dreading what might spew forth presently.

Letting out a harsh breath, I attempt once again to let go of that train of thought and enjoy the pleasantness of the air. It's warm throughout most of the day at this time of year but not quite sweltering. Up to this point, I've been taking advantage of that fact by timing my outer perimeter patrols to the late afternoon shift on most days. When it's quiet like this, with no others about to fracture the silence, you can almost pretend the world is still right.

With a snort, I shake my head in disgust at the concept of 'right.' Heh. That term I'd never apply to our lives and this situation.

I catch the russet flair of a hawk's tail as it cuts through the sky in a sharp dive. Its shrill cry of victory or failure follows me along the outer wall of our hidey hole. I casually light the stub of my second smoke of the day and follow the building's shadow. The sun has begun to descend, following its daily arc above us, throwing most everything on this side of the camp in deeper shades of blue and mauve. It doesn't bother me as I'm more focused on my intended destination.

A row of stacked, large wooden crates, like those used for shipping produce, comes into view. The planks that make up each box's side are warped and fraying from a mix of age and being continuously exposed to desert elements. Rusty nail heads peek out of their driven spots, one after another giving the 'fence' a tetanus shot-required rusticity. A seemingly haphazard barrier runs parallel to the concrete side of the building, about ten feet out and coming just above my head. The office structure composes the other side of the enclosure. We chose this wall for its lack of windows or doors, as it is at the rear of the building.

I keep my steps light as I carefully tread its perimeter, not wanting to disturb what's inside. Regardless of my stealth, I hear shuffling and low sounds—almost moans, though more wistful and pleasant. After 20 feet or so, I reach the end of the manufactured wall, where it turns an abrupt right angle, ending flush with the complex. This shorter side is missing its top stack of crates, allowing the occupants of the enclosed space to be visible but still contained. Beyond the makeshift gate are a pair of big, brown soulful eyes staring unblinkingly at me. I stare right back, though more in curious wonderment than anything else.

The creature before me is not new to either myself or this world. Unafraid, it raises a broad, fuzzy snout, complete with a pair of nostrils that flare as it takes in my scent. Grabbing the tip of a sheathed finger between my front teeth, I pull off the tan glove and set it to the side. Hesitantly, I hold my bare hand in the space between myself and the bull. When no reaction occurs, neither good nor bad, I take it as a sign to proceed. Bare fingertips graze the tan hide, dappled white of a shoulder as it turns its attention back to the grass beneath its cloven feet. The hide is smooth and soft as I trail my fingers along its shorn surface. The yellowed horns crowning its broad skull are equally smooth, though they end in a wicked point that I steer clear of. A reminder that nature tends not to leave its children completely defenseless.

Those silly ribbons from earlier are tied in a series of knots between the twin, keratin-coated horns. I'm half-tempted to pull off the atrocious add-ons, but I stay my hand. I'm sure there must be a reason for the oddity on the oxen and their wagon. I need to remember to ask about their reasoning. At the very least, it should make for a stimulating dinner conversation.

Chewing amiably on the food our interlopers tossed into their quarters, the animal endures my petting without complaint or concern. Cattle are not my favorite animal, that is for certain. They're too massive and smelly, although I can see where others tend to fall for their large doe eyes. However, this beast of burden is warm, soft, and pliant. Its kind face shows no malice or aggression. Not much intelligence either, but frankly, not everything or everyone uses their intelligence appropriately.

Smiling softly, I continue to caress the beast, growing bolder as I map out its eye ridges, horns, and the flat space between its muzzle and the flare of its nostrils. I memorize all I can from this being, not knowing when I'll ever have the opportunity to do so again. Its pelt is short and creamy tan in color. The other half of the pair is charcoal gray—dark enough to look black in low lighting.

Animals as companions are a luxury in the United Forces. Zeta soldiers don't require warm, fuzzy pets or therapy friends.

The only non-human remotely allowed in the UF are canine soldiers, and they and their handlers are restricted to their assigned base. They are not for Zeta soldier excursions that routinely run the risk of encountering the Zee. Dogs can become clandestine carriers, transferring the Zee virus through their fluids and secretions to any human unfortunate enough to make contact. No, when on base perimeter duty with their handler, they function as an organic alarm system, capable of keying in on inhuman presences faster than enhanced soldiers. You just can't beat evolutionary adaptation.

My Comms chirp as I finish giving the steer I've dubbed "Ralph" a final rub and pat on its considerable girth. Leaning back, I depress the receive button and hail whoever is contacting me.

"Omega here. What's up?"

"Oh. Hey, Omega." I wince at Omicron's chipper voice. A happy medic is an unreal, foreboding thing. Giving my full attention to the call, I do my best not to react to the unexpected mood swing.

"Hi, Omicron. What can I help you with?"

I wince, fully expecting to be reamed for something. Nothing like a surprise call from your medic to clear your conscious. Have I done anything wrong lately? Jeopardized my health or the health of someone else? Maybe I shouldn't have punched Tau—not where Omicron could witness it.

Chuckling, Om continues in the same pleasant tone.

"Nothing much. Just wondering if you'd like a couple of pieces of jerky before Mu eats it all."

In the background of Omicron's Comms, I hear Mu's indignant "I did NOT eat all of it! There's plenty left, Omega."

Smiling at the sniper's continued protests and thinking of something other than freeze-dried bricks to eat, I readily agree. After brushing the dirt and hairs from my fingertips, I give the cattle a quick wave goodbye before making tracks to Omicron.

FALLING INTO LINE

I don't even make it to our designated front entrance. After barely going a few steps, something abruptly brings me to a halt. The air has a strange tang to it. I detect some kind of greenery— crisp, fresh, and earthy, like freshly trimmed grass in the spring. Following the initial whiff, I promptly recognize two things. One, I'm not alone, and two, that nature-packed smell can only come from the Alpha. My mouth draws down without intending to.

My newly dubbed nemesis, Tau, is waiting for me, dark scorn in place.

I can't seem to help my gut reaction to this guy. Not that his reception to me is any better. Without a sound, he steps into the fading outside light. He's feeling less than courteous towards me at the moment if that thin-lipped scowl is anything to go by. I guess laying into him earlier didn't earn me any brownie points. Not that I care to endear myself to him.

At that thought, I smirk, eyes flashing dangerously at his dour person. Two can play this game.

"Can I help you with something, Tau?" That's about as civil as he's going to get from me.

His lines around his mouth deepen further, and the thick rule of his dark brows draws down entirely. On his nearly hairless face, I can easily spot the fading, fist-sized bruise I gifted him along the left jawline. By tomorrow evening, no mark will be left for any to see. It's unfair. That was a good hit.

His fully-suited up self shifts imperceptibly to the right, and I follow the gesture on automatic before comprehending. The stoic man appears uncomfortable, and now I know why. Smirk back at full power, I can't resist goading him.

"Ah. I see. Sneaking around, then? Maybe hoping to get some juicy gossip from my team. No? How about our guests?"

That gets a better reaction. Tau's face flushes a vivid and blotchy red, readily apparent on his smoothly shaved and fairer complexion. The soldier bares his teeth in a mockery of a snarl, and my hackles rise in anticipation.

"Mind your own business, woman! It's irresponsible enough that you allowed civilians into a United Forces camp. You have also given them unfettered access to your soldiers and equipment. Who knows what they have gotten into and overheard?"

"It's not against regulations to temporarily house civilians, provided protecting them doesn't conflict with an existing directive. What good are we as Zeta soldiers if we can't protect those who need it?" I'm practically growling in response.

"Not to mention," I continue without pause, "that my team has kept them under a tight watch. They haven't had free access to any place or person in this camp."

Now equally red in the face, I feel caught off guard by his accusation. I shouldn't be. We are perfectly within our prerogative to have offered those girls some semblance of safety. Regardless, I feel compelled to defend my decision. I don't doubt that it's the right one to have made.

"Perhaps not. But your second did take one of those young women on a joy ride on his ATC."

The Alpha sadly makes a fair point, but he's also putting his prominent nose into matters that aren't his business. Eyes narrowing, my right-hand forms a fist before I tamp down the flare of emotion. Breathing in once through the nose, then out in a loud huff, I try to be reasonable.

"I've already handled any sensitive information or issues. We aren't some green team with no experience dealing with civvies. My people know their duties, as well as their priorities."

Arms crossed over an armored chest, he sternly stares me down. I seethe internally caught off guard by one of my team. Damn that Rho. If what Tau says is true, he's getting a few more jobs on top of what I've already assigned him as punishment. That, and a thorough ass-chewing. Sadly, there's little reason not to believe that my second stepped out of line for a cotton-garbed bootie call. I have to concede to that.

"If that's the case, he will be dealt with. Regardless, he's of my concern and not yours." Stepping closer, I intentionally move into his personal space.

"You need to watch yourself. The only reason you're with my team is that we have no choice in the matter. Our orders are to keep you alive in so far as we can. Obviously, I need to remind you that yours is to aid my team on missions and follow my command."

From this close, I can see his perfectly straight white teeth gnash as garnet eyes flash in anger. I don't budge when he presses forward, and all but looms in my space. Funny, the dude isn't that much taller than me. I guess it's his general presence that gives the impression otherwise. Probably a result of his Asian heritage. I'd say he's Japanese-ish if I were to guess.

As he shifts and all but snarls at me, I catch sight of an intricately woven violet handle sticking straight out over his shoulder. A katana's handle. Thank you, anime, for the reference point. Definitely Japanese, then.

"You have no right to order me. I know my place, Beta. You should know yours."

"Yeah. Well, fuck you and your hierarchy fixation. If you don't want to deal with me or my orders, you can leave." I nod my head behind me in emphasis.

That gives him pause, like soldier boy never thought to go outside his issued orders. Funny, considering technically, he was AWOL for a portion of the time. I guess the return to good health means a return to abiding by the rules.

"Hmph. I have no intent to disregard orders from our headquarters," is his low rejoinder. He recrosses his arms sharply and turns his head away in unison. I fight the itch to poke him in the face, just for the hell of it. That or sock him another one. He could use a new bruise.

"I'm sure you don't, and neither do I."

Sighing, I finally take a step back and stop bristling at him.

"Look, this isn't ideal for either of us, but we both have a duty to the UF to uphold. I will do my job and take care of my team. You are unfortunately included in that for the time being."

His deep red eyes soften as he looks away, and I think I may have reached him. Heh, not so. In the next instant, he shutters himself and practically screams at me.

"I don't need taking care of. Not by you or anyone else on this ridiculous team!"

Without another word, Tau turns in a flash of a gunmetal gray cloak and stomps out of the room in a tiff.

I wait until I no longer hear the echo of his steps before giving in to my earlier urge. The satisfying sting that ricochets from knuckles to brain brings a stark clarity to my immediate world. I needed that. Something to bring me down from that precipice of rage and anger lurking below the surface. Have I mentioned that Zeta soldiers tend towards violence more than your average Joe?

Shaking my head and feeling disgusted. I don't inspect the reaction any further to determine who exactly it's for. There are times when diving deeper into emotions causes more harm than otherwise.

PRIME RIBS AND
CHOICE CONVERSATIONS

A bsently, I chew on the meat from some critter that Omicron managed to skin, cook the hell out of, and make into a decent jerky. I don't bother asking what it is anymore. There's enough fat banded throughout to make the dried stick kind of chewy and about as tender as it can be in its desiccated state.

In no time, my snack is gone, allowing my attention to focus on the girl I believe to be the youngest of our squatters. The jubilant brunette named Anne dances from the side of the bottom floor, where the clean water is collected and stored, to the row of sleeping mats placed by the solid back wall. The other women are already gathered there, sitting amongst their meager possessions. They all seem comfortable and at home in our space. I would say nomadic life and shacking up with strangers is commonplace for all of them.

My precarious perch high in the rickety rafters of our warehouse allows me to become a silent observer of the newcomers below. The bonus is the few precious moments of silence and isolation I gain. These minor things translate to peace and joy in my pathetic little world.

Thankfully, I did not budge about the oxen being part of the possessions they could house inside. I draw a clear division about sleeping with livestock. Between us and the cattle, the Zee can have them. It's bad enough having little to no modern conveniences without adding the aroma of musty pelt and fresh manure to the mix.

The mocha-skinned femme with strong opinions appears docile for the moment. There's a rhythmic rustle of thick locks of hair shifting as Kari plaits Goldilocks' (AKA Janet's) hair into a neat, single braid. Anne is chattering about who knows what in the background to anyone who will listen. I don't think that girl has taken a break from the continuous speech she's issued since they followed us home. She could give Mu a challenge in verbosity. It's beyond me how this group of happy-go-lucky individuals has managed to remain among the living, at least from outward appearances.

Snorting in disbelief, I run the tip of my tongue along my front teeth, clearing up any bits of snack left. Straightening up slowly from my hunkered-down pose, I hold back a groan as everything realigns and settles within. I'm not old. Not by any standard means of defining it. I have been doing this shit for almost a decade, and the scars of this life are carved deep into the hollow of me. And I'm not referring to the rents left behind in my flesh from teeth and nails or the odd red splotches scattered over my body as reminders of the various projectiles forced through without hesitation.

What happens to a person when they're forced to kill their kind? Over and over, again and again. The aftermath of being a long-term exterminator of the former human race has never been studied, let alone acknowledged as a potential issue by the UF.

I'm sure my employer is banking on all Zeta soldiers' natural and eventual extinction before it becomes a bullet point on some to-do list. It's simply a matter of who or what will deal a death blow. The Zee, a marauder, or even well-meaning folk might bring about our end. In attempting to remove one evil, we've created a second that was never intended to coexist with humankind.

I can recall a handful of times I witnessed when the transition to Zeta soldier didn't work out as planned. What resulted…the thing that was left…never remained long. The echo of multiple weapons discharged in near synchronicity still cracks loudly across my memories. There's no way I can allow that to happen to either myself or my team. I vowed this to myself long ago and will not be swayed. Ever. The day may come when we wish for our end, but it will be by choice. The ability to choose a path for oneself is rare in this line of work. As changed as Zeta soldiers are, we're still human. We're not mindless beasts. At least not for now.

Stepping softly, I make my way along the beam to where it T-sections with a matte gray stucco wall. I drop down to the floor below the top two levels of this derelict building with a light hop, landing delicately on the pads of my feet and fingertips. My sudden drop is a damn near silent landing. Not that it matters, as the applause of a single individual immediately meets me. My self-satisfaction turns into a look to rival a grumpy cat.

Straightening to my entire 5 foot and some change height, I pass a glare over my shoulder to the slender form leaning casually against a girder like some lounging cat. Chi exudes smugness. It's pretty much her modus operandi.

"That truly was skillful, Omega. What were you doing up there? Pretending to be a Nosferatu? You have the dark and skulking part down, at the minimum."

Given that I've gotten a consistent six hours of sleep the last few nights, I'm less inclined to react to her poking. It's best to let her comments roll off of me, in any case. This entity is a bored Chi I'm interacting with, to be sure. Not so rare a critter as the 'happy Chi,' but still a couple of steps to the side of her normal state. I've learned that the leggy demolition lady tends to poke and harass others when she lacks other things to occupy her attention. During the first part of our tenure together, her sniping would lead to a very embarrassing reaction on my part. All decorum was non-existent, with my prickly and cocky self in full effect. I may still behave that way if she keeps it up, but as I previously stated, I'm well-rested and, therefore, in a not-so-bad mood.

Turning fully and leveling a look her way, I finally respond. "Is there something that I can help you with, Chi?"

Flicking a bare, manicured hand out for inspection, she doesn't bother to give me her full attention.

"Well, as entertaining as our new guests have been, I have to say their overall mannerisms and conversation leave something to be desired. Any chance we'll be vacating these premises sometime in the near future?"

The column of my neck itches to be cracked, so I indulge in a shoulder roll before replying.

"You know about as much as I do. We're in a holding pattern until HQ finishes rearranging our schedule. The UF is looking for ways to fast-track the tiresome Alpha's return while still having us get a shitload done on the way."

Her thin lips form a delicate pout for a moment before her expression smooths into its usual poker face.

"That's a shame. I would not mind a distraction beyond these ancient and gray walls."

"What? Our accommodations don't meet your standards, princess? Why don't you discuss your disparagement with the Alpha? I'm sure he'd love to harangue along with you."

Good humor gone, she wrinkles her nose in distaste at my sarcasm. There are times when I get glimpses of who Chi was before she became a soldier. We wouldn't have run in the same social circle, let alone ZIP code. It begs the question of how and why she decided to join the United Forces. Let alone why the violet-locked lady would submit herself to becoming a Zeta soldier. I'm not one to poke into people's private lives, though, so I've never asked, and she's never offered.

Taking in her now dour expression and lack of delight, I opt for the higher road and extend an olive branch of sorts.

Scratching a non-existent itch, I ask nonchalantly, "Is there something that you need to talk with me about, Chi?"

Shaking her short, stick-straight violet locks, some of her temper abates. Her lips are almost ghost-white, pursed as she mentally chews on whatever is floating around in that clinically calculating mind of hers. She almost starts twice before she finally gives in and shares whatever is eating at her.

"I accidentally read one of our guests."

My eyebrows have probably disappeared into my hairline with surprise. Chi's usually extremely cautious about whose mind she telepathically rifles through. My demo specialist must be distracted to allow such a lapse to occur.

I don't bother hiding my eagerness to hear whatever she's uncovered. I had a keen fascination with the human mind before everything went slantways. Sometimes I would much rather have Chi's inherent gift than my own. Seeing another person's innermost sanctum sounds valuable and intriguing, provided you can stand the individual. From what she's told me, the amount of mental discipline required is potentially more than I have at my disposal. Curiosity is a dangerous thing for someone with what amounts to textbook telepathy.

Not losing the opportunity to inner musings, I quickly ask, "So, what did you find?"

Nose crinkling in either thought or distaste, she puts up a fraction of hesitation before giving in. It must be bad if she's not making me beg or whine for it.

"They're not lying when they say there is a nomadic band in the area they seek. They failed to mention that they're also looking for a particular location near where we are. They seem to think of themselves as part of some holy and higher calling. That they will somehow save humanity." Chi shares, quiet and careful.

"Say what?" I'm surprised by that. "Do you mean they're intentionally wandering around here without set coordinates, hoping to run across someplace purely by divine chance?"

"That's exactly what I mean. It appears these women chose to veer from their original destination to find this someone or something. They've tied a lot of importance and urgency to whatever it is."

"You're kidding me, right? Well, that explains a few things. It also begs the question of what exactly they're seeking."

"Gauging their true purpose was vague at best—more ethereal to my read." Chi's eyes narrow in what I take to be frustration on her part. "I could not get them to fixate long enough on the thought to get a clearer picture. It was strange. Usually, when a person has a goal, it is at the forefront of their mind."

"Interesting." Rubbing my chin, I contemplate the lack of disclosure. It's unusual for my spy not to pull some helpful nugget in her readings. It further contributes to the puzzle that is these four women. "We're missing something. They are in the middle of nowhere, unarmed and seemingly unconcerned with the general state of the world around them."

"Yes, that seems a bit…?"

"Odd?"

Chi snorts. "I was going to say 'stupid,' actually."

I give a wry grin in agreement. Not that I've ever heard Chi call someone "stupid" outright. It's probably beneath her.

I'm prepared to expound upon that thread of thought when I get sidetracked. That term 'holy order' shakes some memory loose from the dark annals of my mind.

"You know, I've heard something like a holy order mentioned before. I think in passing from one of the other Zeta squads."

I rack my brain trying to put solid words to that vague idea. All the while, my aloof companion's eyes follow me with the amusement one reserves for lesser beings. I can only guess that this mystery of our guests has also piqued her interest. Then, I recall it so clearly I feel foolish for having misplaced the thought. A long-forgotten aside made by another Beta captain. Nameless to me and of minor importance, save that he had a nice smile, and I may or may not have had temporary relations with him.

"There's some group that made an appearance around five years ago," I hedge. "They claim to be their God's 'chosen ones.' The "Children of the Light" or the "Light of Life"? Something to that effect. Those spared the Zee plague, both during and after. They're supposed to be tasked with some grand design by the Almighty."

I glance at Chi, and I'm met with a blank face.

"What? I'm just repeating what I was told," I comment sharply. "The long and short is that they've taken their unaltered humanity as a sign that they are meant for greater things."

Finger on her chin, Chi looks thoughtful. "Well, I guess they would not be the first to take cheating death by what is a pure chance to mean they can assign a higher value to themselves than others. Most of us aspire to be more than a simple waste of carbon."

"Is that all we are in the end?" I muse softly, more to myself than the demo chick.

"Depends on who you ask." She shrugs indifferently. "Frankly, it doesn't matter much in the end. We all eventually become the dust of our world, feeding the next generation of life."

"That's rather Buddhist of you," I can't help but tease.

Philosophical Chi is always a laugh to be around. Definitely up there in the rare occurrences category, and two in one day? Fascinating.

"Hardly," she sharply intones. The general feeling of warmth and mirth vanishes instantly as she closes herself off again. Ah. I must have touched a sensitive subject. Good mood lost then. I don't take it personally. I've always found Chi to be tetchy about random issues and private about herself in all dimensions. A change of topic is needed, then.

"So, in your professional opinion, should we be concerned about these women?"

"Not entirely. There is no hint of malice or aggression that I have observed in any manner. Then again, zealots are fanatical."

"Okay…so leery as always with the strange strangers. Got it. Can you be so kind as to spread that carefully to the others?"

Sighing, I rub my head tiredly, "As usual, I'll check in with HQ in the next couple of hours. I think it's worth mentioning this to them and our current location to be safe."

No sense in getting caught unawares by some unassuming waifs, particularly if they end up being a more significant threat than we know. That would be an awful mark on my personnel record.

"Will do, Omega."

Dark head down, she brushes past me, disappearing into the shadows just as quickly as she appeared. I'm about to do the same when I pick up a murmur. Tilting my head to better capture the sound, I pick up at least two voices. They're doing their best not to project whatever they're discussing.

It's probably a smart move by the UF not to advertise the overall extent of enhanced senses that Zeta soldiers are endowed with. Hell, I've even heard mention of some new-gen soldiers with senses beyond the standard upgrade—subsonic hearing and vision that allows them to see as far as an eagle. While questionably plausible, those particular talents are not impossible overall.

Regardless, it's an oversight on their part that they happen to be temporarily cohabiting with six highly trained Zeta soldiers. That was a big mistake on their part. Whoever it is, they've been overheard, and I want to know what's worth hiding.

A SIMMERING POT

S liding as flatly as possible along the wall, I creep to where the voices originate. Back rubbing against the irregular texture of unfinished concrete walls, I can still sense someone else's physical presence. My breath barely leaves my body as I strain to pick up on the conversation a room over and several floors below. The large floorplan of this place no longer seems like the bonus I initially thought it was. These spaces are too open. Too exposed. Too mid-century ultra-modern.

I overhear three things almost immediately: "survivors," "soldiers," and something about "horde," but that's all. I'm still too far away to decipher what's being said. Both speakers are feminine, and I have no trouble ruling out the other two females on my team. Living in close proximity for this long breeds a certain level of familiarity.

Head cocked to the side, I try to catch a little more but am disappointed. They're too damn far away, and the more I attempt to pick up on their conversation, the less I feel that I'm hearing.

Eyes darting from the crumbling wall, exposed floorboards, and precariously hanging safety signage, I grit my teeth as no good options present themselves. I need somewhere I can hopefully listen in unobserved. I take in the distinct lack of places to conceal myself with. Aha! I can't help the grin as my gaze lands on an exposed I-beam jutting from the third floor.

I can work with that. It's almost directly above the cluster and a better observation spot. This part of the warehouse only receives light from a set of small windows along the furthest side. Couple that with a mostly intact roof, and the resulting area is shrouded in shadow. Of course, it can't be that easy. To get to such a perfect position, I'll have to move across an open space, employing some acrobatics along the way. All the while hopefully not being noticed by our guests.

As I shift on my feet in thought, the light jingle of my vest reminds me that I'm not precisely stealthy in my current state. After hesitating while grinding my teeth in indecision, I give in and strip off extraneous gear and weaponry.

It's a bitch to unbuckle things quietly, but I manage to place the various metal, hard plastic, and leather pieces in a neat stack on the ground where I stand. My disrobing down to just uniform and sidearms takes no more than a minute, but I distinctly feel that loss of attention toward what they're saying. Their conversation will be over long before I get my ass into position at this rate. Satisfied with my stripped-down state, I'm off and sprinting in long strides across the floor, from one side of the room to the other.

My initial leap gets me up to the third floor. After a few more seconds of free climbing a pillar, I get to where I want to be. Body poised on all fours, my breaths come in light pants as I tilt my head, straining to detect if they noticed me. They continue uninterrupted by my presence.

"Did you find them?"

"Not entirely. I think we're close."

"That's good. It means we'll be able to leave this area sooner than we originally expected. Are the others close?"

"I think so. I didn't want to worry anyone, but our food and water were quite low. Fortunately, we ran across these soldiers when we did."

Standing there, listening from afar, in so much as I can tell, they haven't heard or seen me. I'm not surprised. Even with my enhanced vision, I still have difficulty perceiving them across the length of the dimmed space.

"Yes. One might say it's more than fortuitous. We should be thankful for the mercy and kindness they bestowed upon us." That one is Morgan. I recognize her tone now and her unique way of speaking. Who talks like that anymore?

"True. Oh! Have you been able to speak to any of these folk? I wonder what they are doing out here." The second speaker reveals herself to be the younger redhead, Kari.

"No, I have not had much of an opportunity thus far. They seem to keep to their schedules and are rarely alone. Mealtime is the only occasion I've seen them socialize casually with each other. It makes it difficult to speak with them one-on-one."

"Well, I've spent a little time with that cute, taller one. You know, Rho?"

Here the respondent giggles, and I realize a third person has joined the conversation. Janet. Her words give me a distinct 'uh-oh feeling' in my gut, as my mama liked to call it. Somehow I know where this conversation is heading. Insert another tittering giggle here from the brunette. Ugh.

"Oh, he's just so sweet and funny. An absolute darling. I can't believe he's a soldier. If it weren't for the clothes, I would never have guessed. What a gentleman. I feel bad for him being stuck here without contact in these dreadful times."

There's a mournful sound in response, and I roll my eyes at their naivety. Puh-lease. Rho thrives on our little setup. I'm sure he's already working the 'lonely hero' angle. Seriously. I will have to punch him—twice—in the nuts for good measure.

"At least there's the comfort of our company for now. That's the best we can provide to any of them." The eldest sagely adds.

"Indeed. And the right thing for us to do." The wink thrown in at the end by the resident flirt of their group is nearly audible. Okay. I've heard enough.

I'm about to vacate the space when a thought occurs to me. I blatantly realize the fourth and youngest of their party has yet to show herself. Well, isn't that convenient...and suspicious. Where the hell is she? Chi has patrol of camp, so she should have some inkling as to the goings-on of the interior. I wonder if that's the femme she read? I'll need to check in with her privately as soon as possible.

Glancing back to the huddle of women, I surmise there can't be much left of value for them to discuss. No sense hanging around. Leaning away from the space, I can't help my snort of derision. Figures that my second would end up a part of the gossip. That scruffy-faced dude is far too predictable.

Sighing, I inadvertently take in the mustier air that liberally coats this part of the office complex. It's the type of building design made popular towards the end of the century. All communal shared working spaces that individuals can drop into and set up their personal workstations or use an open one for a short period. Handy for a mostly remote workforce where meeting in the flesh is old-fashioned and unsanitary.

We chose to house ourselves on the westward side partially for the solid walls and roof but even more for the airflow and fresher grounds. This vector seems to have some underlying funk with no apparent origin. It's not just the nailed shut and glued windows contributing to the issue. I have a feeling that there may be other factors at work. Considering we'll only be visiting another day or two, I don't feel like exploring the 'whys' and 'wherefores.' We need to clean up and move on to our resupply.

"Food's ready!"

Mu's voice filters through the brief break in the women's discussion, serving to end my thoughts. I can visualize the shorter stride she tends towards as brisk footsteps herald her entrance. They also result from the seeming constant excitement that infuses her very being. My point is summarily proven as she bursts into the room in a flurry of energy and movement.

"Oh, there you are!" The girls startle slightly at her sudden appearance, apparently too engrossed in their conversation to be aware of their surroundings. The sniper isn't fazed by their reaction. No doubt an intentional act on her part to set them at ease. Mu has always been good at reading the room. She is a very empathetic human and as mindful of the feelings of others as you can get. I don't know how she still manages to be that way as a veteran soldier. The two roles are opposites to me, with no overlap or in-between. Even now, those luminous cyan eyes are taking in our guests. An openness and eagerness to engage with others pours forth from her—a behavior reserved purely for those extroverted types. She's much better at these person-to-person interactions than I've ever been.

The eldest recovers first and responds to Mu with in-kind enthusiasm. Whether or not it's contrived is challenging to tell from afar.

"Hello there. Mew, is it?"

"Yup! That's me. I just wanted to let you girls know we're serving dinner in just a few if you're hungry. We have a habit of being very timely with our meals." She rounds out the invite with a broad grin.

The other four females melt at her antics, and she's met with warm regard. Wait, four? Yup. I catch the final female slipping in from the side, joining the other women as if she was always there. I note that they do not even shift in reaction to her presence, as if they were expecting her to slip in late. Seems like there's definitely something there. For now, I shift my attention back to the current interactions and leave the unknown to be dealt with later.

I immediately glom onto the fact that although Mu's wearing her standard UF flak jacket, there's a noticeable lack of rifle and sidearm. My chapped lips contort, torn between anger and frustration at her oversight. Technically, we're never unarmed in the literal sense, but a skinny, 5-foot-plus girl like Mu will appear weak and vulnerable based on standard human assumptions. I've used that same misperception and prejudice to my advantage in a fight. My team needs to project an overall impression of strength and unity.

In the now waning light, Mu's heritage and Zeta enhancement contrast sharply with the civvies around her. Her smooth skin is that lovely shade of hazelnut brown that I've always associated with people of Indian heritage. However, the chances of having the inhumanly blue pigmentation of her irises from her Indian descent are doubtful, as is having glow-in-the-dark eyes. I understand that they go a long way toward enhancing night vision. If my sharp-sighted gunner lingers much longer, she'll be treating our guests to just how unnatural Zeta soldiers can be.

Frankly, I have never gotten used to it. I am, however, not as obvious about it as I was at first. I think between the staring and the yelping when caught unawares. I may have hurt Mu's overflowing feelings in the beginning. She's still a little sensitive about being the blue-eyed monster in a sea of crimson. Our eyes are just one of those spectacular, unexpected side effects of experimenting with the human genome.

Warning! Becoming a Zeta soldier may result in a few quirks, such as super-human strength and the heightened desire to consume animal protein. And, of course, the most unnatural, reddest eyes you've ever seen.

I lean against the pillar behind me as Mu ushers the pack of females toward our inner sanctum. No doubt it's Omicron's fabulous field cooking we're being treated to. I'm not joking, either. The guy can do amazing things with a bit of salt, pepper, and a lizard.

As Mu moves to exit the space, steering the other two ahead, she glances at my position, raising a bisected eyebrow. I respond in kind and stick out my tongue for good measure. I'll follow suit shortly, but I will enjoy this moment of solitude. I don't need to be first in the chow line.

A low gurgle from my midsection does remind me that some sustenance in the near future isn't the worst idea. I'm sure I missed lunch between my routine patrol around our camp and the additional recon I've assigned to myself concerning our new house guests. The scent of something spicy, grilled, and altogether beautiful wafts through the open space. Leaning back on my haunches, I rub my grumbling and impatient stomach, soothing it back to dormancy. Soon, my precious. There's a severe calorie deficit that I need to make up for. No sense in wasting away while I'm on the job.

Taking a last, deep inhale of whatever is on the menu, I rise to a standing position and eyeball the space between myself and the landing a story below. Deeming it doable, I engage the thick muscles of my thighs in an all-out sprint, leaping across the gap and down a floor. I land with the grace of a gymnast right where I intended, hands bracing my form.

See, Mom? The military can teach you a respectable skill beyond killing and familial abandonment. I was as clumsy as a baby rhino as a child and didn't do much better as a teenager. It was a relief to come into this world a second time with an innate sense of balance and agility. Talk about a confidence booster.

Brushing my gloved hands against each other, I clear stucco and splinters from the outside of the worn material. There's a dinner I need to attend, among other things. My weapons and poncho are still exactly where I left them, untouched.

With the weight of my gear settled back in place, I casually make my way toward the sounds of the others. The walls are now all dim and gray as evening settles in. Air moves by my face in a gentle caress bringing that out-of-place smell along with it. Glancing into the gloaming one last time, I can't help but wonder at its source. Maybe I don't want to know?

TAKING THINGS IN HAND

W hy did I think eating together was a good idea? That self-pitying thought is echoing around the chamber of my mind. Choking down the sponge-like substance of supposed Mom's Meatloaf (MRE labels don't lie), I feel a bit queasy, and it's not the food. It's my subordinate as he interacts with the civvies—Rho's in his full glory and on display for all. Whimsical stories seem to spew forth as he shifts closer to the fair-haired girl on his left, then leans in the opposite direction to include the ginger female on his right in whatever yarn he's spinning. All the while, he's cross-legged and bouncing his ocean-colored dinner plate on a long thigh.

Shaking my head reluctantly, I glance over to where my indigo-haired sniper is and have to blink hard at the sight. She's completely absorbed in her meal, or so it seems. As the slim gunner's voice loudly becomes a rowdy bark of a laugh, she hunches down more, almost as if she's trying to fold in on herself and avoid notice. With hair as short as hers, there's no hiding her expression. Plus, it's unlikely she'll escape notice from the rest of the team, given how observant they are, except for the chortling and oblivious long-faced male who tends to miss the world outside himself. In the end, Rho comes first for Rho. All other concerns are secondary.

The hard crunch of air-fried carrot sticks is loud to my ears. I've moved on in courses (and consistencies) from bland mush to overly salted and crunchy twigs. It'd be great if whoever planned our meals bothered to take in the entire Gestalt and not simply check off the nutrition-only aspect. I guess I was wrong, thinking Omicron had a tasty supper prepared for us. The lack of appealing entrees is part of why I'd take his barbecued rodent over any military meal plan. I had to hold back the tears when I learned that those tasty morsels of meat went primarily to our guests.

Damn him for feeling overly generous with his edible food.

Speak of the devil, Om's seated to my right, chatting amicably with Chi. Both are relaxed and keen to ignore the drama taking place across from our slice of the circle. It's an interesting dynamic between my blow-it-up girl and fix-'em-now man. Those two have always shared an easy camaraderie. Not so different from what I had with my former second, Eps. Something about his nature and mine led us to have a quick and deep trust and, later, a solid and dependable friendship. Maybe it's not so different from what I have with Rho sometimes if I'm candid about icky feelings. And, of course, the shaved head and sullen countenance of Tau lurks just beyond those two.

Thankfully, our twittering guests decided to sit on the other side of our resident Alpha, so I escaped having to share proximity with the guy (or them) right now. Taking a particularly vicious bite of my hard-as-a-rock carrot stick, I allow my loathing for him to simmer for a moment. Then, I become a responsible adult and rein it back in like a good little soldier. No sense projecting hostility in mixed company or a lack of cohesiveness as a unit. I prefer to play it close to the chest.

I suck the last salt crystals from my fingers and brush my palms off. Rising smoothly without making eye contact, I efficiently grab my meal gear and head to the wash basin. The mindless habit is great for times like this when my inner introvert screams loud and clear for personal space. It seems that my 'fuck off' vibe is broadcasting quite well to everyone around me, with no hint of misinterpretation.

Chore completed. It's time for the last task of the day: guard assignments. Whoopie.

There's been a leisurely attitude within my team of late, including the plus one. It's not as though anyone has become lax in their duties, but they are tending toward slower response times and taking longer doing the same responsibilities required of us. It's time to move on to our next assignment.

Doing a quick mental review, I select today's assignments based on last night's rotation. The benefit of being in charge—I can arrange things such that the asshole and I are not on the same shift most of the time. I can grant my de facto second that dubious honor. Turning around to face my seated teammates, I try not to give away my deviousness.

"Okay, Rho and Tau, you two are on the first shift."

There's a curse and a groan. I'm not sure those sounds came from the same person.

"Next will be Mu and Chi. Omicron and I will round out the night. That's three-hour shifts each if anyone is unclear?"

There's a slew of moans to rival the Zee, but blessedly no verbal arguments. That slight lack of decorum rankles me, particularly on display as it is in front of the civvies. Little did I know that the skills I learned babysitting children during high school would help me out much later during my illustrious military career. A pesky lock of hair flops into my eye, and I irritably brush it aside before giving my assembled team a "no buts" look to make it clear that I'm unimpressed with their whining.

With that settled, the rustle of fabric draws my attention to the four others in our midst. The eldest looks bemused while the three younger girls try to follow what is happening on our side of the Kumbaya circle. I figure now is a good time to deal with my expectations for the evening.

"My people will be on shift throughout the night. I ask that you keep to your sleeping area once night falls to prevent any mishaps or unfortunate accidents."

We're on a hairpin trigger at the best of times, so having some civvie wandering around is liable to result in someone dying. I place my bet on that being the nubile and clueless ones.

"What if something happens during the night?" Blondie voices as she glances slyly toward Rho. I can sense him taking a breath that will herald some ridiculous statement.

"We're a team of highly trained, enhanced soldiers. Believe me, if your breathing so much as hitches during sleep, we'll know." My eyebrows draw down in a sharp "V," I think my glare gets the message across to her.

She shrinks back slightly at my tone, and I let that statement sink into the rest of the room for a moment. I may not explicitly threaten them, but they'd better watch themselves around our camp. The last thing I want is for someone to get the idea that they can pull a fast one on my team.

As a look passes between them, I fish a flimsy toothpick out of my vest and wedge it behind my left incisor. They're the minty kind, so I can grind on one for a short time and have okay breath for a few minutes. Hard to be overly hygienic during the end of days.

"Understood," Morgan intones solemnly, meeting my expression with an equally serious one.

Good. Message received by that one.

I offer her a minimal smile as she straightens up, brushing nonexistent crumbs from the deep folds of her gray pants. She nods once before indicating for the others to clean and return their dishes before shepherding the lot back to their designated space. Those who remain seated exchange their looks before cleaning up and clearing out.

I get a muffled "spoilsport" from Rho as he passes. I shrug it off with the same indifference as I receive from Tau.

At least Mu bequeaths a broad smile upon me as she gets ready to head upstairs, no doubt to get cleaned up and settled in. That girl probably has an acquired book from the last time we were back at the base between missions. Stashed somewhere in her gear to be consumed whenever free time presents itself. Speaking of books, I wonder if she has an extra one I can borrow. No sense wasting the opportunity.

ALARMS AND THE ALARMING

Someone is scratching at the wall near my head, and they'd better cut that shit. That's the first thing my tired mind offers me as I break my sleep cycle. It's probably close to when the alarm is set to go off, but early still, I'm certain.

A blurry glance at the clock face embedded in my left gauntlet confirms that. There's more of that almost non-existent sound of scritching and scrabbling. It brings to mind long fingernails running along wooden boards. Damn rodents. With a huff, I give up on the pretense of rest and sit up sharply in my chosen bedding, kicking off the part still covering my legs until my feet are clear. My eyes close for the moment as I rub bare fingers against the short, soft hairs along the nape of my neck, tilting my head to listen.

Almost immediately, I'm aware of a presence nearby. My spy and demo specialist is leaning casually against the drab gray wall closest to my bedding, still and wrapped in shadow.

"Any changes?" I manage to get out to Chi between yawns.

She gives me a smirk but somehow resists teasing me just yet.

With a shift of her hip, a glance is directed toward the center of the building's open middle. From here, I can make out four human-sized mounds on the floor, piled close to each other. In our shared sleeping space, no sound escapes the others apart from the occasional shift of a body or mumble of REM.

"They've been pretty quiet. I saw Omicron at around 0330. He had no incidents to report either. The team seems to be sleeping well, even Tau."

I automatically roll my eyes at the name. The demolitionist shakes her head, exasperation coloring her voice.

"Really, Omega. You'll have to get used to being in proximity to our rescue at some point. We've got him for the next three to four months, right?"

I shudder at that. "Ugh. Don't remind me."

"Yes, well, as you so carefully planned it, you avoided sharing a shift and sparkling conversation with him. Best prepare yourself for the next day's suffering."

With that, she flicks her wrist and turns neatly on her heel.

"I'd rather prepare for a colonoscopy!" I call after her.

I don't know if she hears my parting statement, but it doesn't matter. With a gust of air, I gird my non-existent loins and prepare myself mentally for shift.

As I carefully step towards the center chamber, I opt to pull my poncho on for warmth. Before starting my patrol, I feel a strong urge to perform a quick check of our guests.

My path is circuitous but allows me to assess everything more thoroughly. It also makes it more apparent that something is amiss. One of the girl's ugly sleeping bags looks off compared to the others. I swear if Rho's fucking around…

With a low growl, I stalk over to the anomaly, prepared to rend my second from his favorite limb before stopping short.

Well, this can't be good. That thought is immediate, along with the recognition that, no, that is not a body or bodies lying there. It's a pile of blankets and clothes haphazardly shoved into an empty sleeping bag to look like a body. Well, crap.

Crouching closer to the offending item, I inhale deeply and discover a lack of scent. A light touch confirms the bedding is cool as well.

It seems that our guest has decided to go on an unauthorized twilight adventure. Turning my head slowly to look at the room's other occupants, a stray lock of red falls into my eyes yet again. Damn. My hair is getting too long. Going to have to chop this stuff off. Brushing it aside, I focus on the remaining females. Without getting any closer, it's easy to tell that they are all soundly asleep. The cadence of their breathing and the slower rate of their heartbeats are loud indicators. Sighing softly, I rise on stiff knees and cautiously back out of the area.

With quiet, brisk steps, I make my way to one of the three functioning concrete stairwells remaining in this structure. The fourth looks as though Thor's hammer was dropped directly upon it. Now jogging up the split-level flight, I'm in my team's area within a minute or so. I head straight to where Chi lies, mostly asleep on her side, and give her a quick nudge with the tip of my boot.

"Huh? What, Omega?" She blinks at me in confusion before clarity cascades across her perfectly symmetrical face.

"What's wrong?" Her long form straightens, sitting up immediately.

"We've got a wanderer. The dark-skinned girl, Kari, is missing," I intone lowly, not wanting to disturb the others…yet. "Did you notice anything odd during your shift?"

A look of heavy concentration crosses her features. Chi is a details person, and that may be our saving grace.

"Yes," she begins slowly. "I heard something. Scratching, I thought. I went to inspect it and only saw a rat creeping around. I didn't think anything of it after that. I assumed it was the local vermin."

"I guess that wasn't the only thing creeping around," I mutter, reflecting on the scratching earlier. Perhaps it was not imagined. "Do you recall when that was?"

"0150 or so. I remember because when I glanced at my chrono, it was almost exactly at the hour. So a little more than an hour ago."

"Right."

Slinging my rifle over the shoulder, I extend my free hand to Chi, gesturing for her to rise. Her long, slender fingers grasp mine tightly as I propel her to her feet. I wait impatiently as she meticulously straightens her uniform before redressing in her vest, gauntlets, and shin guards. Weapons are last—hers consisting of a sidearm, a dirk-like dagger, and our standard-issue rifle. Fully geared up, she nods as I make a swift and quiet exit from our team's quarters, running down the stairwell two steps at a time.

Now clear of those with sensitive hearing, I hail our other teammate who's up and about.

"Om, do you read me over?"

"Clearly, Omega, over."

"Good. What's your current position?"

Even as I ask, I'm scanning the room we've entered for any indication as to which way that femme could have gone.

"I'm outside along the western wall. All's clear over here."

"Okay. For now, can you keep to the perimeter? One of our esteemed guests seems to have run off in the night. Chi and I will search the interior, but I need you to keep on the lookout for the darker-skinned one."

"Will do, Omega. Omicron out."

With that taken care of, for the time being, I readdress the soldier standing next to me. There's something amiss here. I can't pinpoint what it is specifically, and the 'why' of it eludes me. Just a hunch that something terrible is about to happen.

"Chi, start at the roof and work your way down. I'll take the ground level and hopefully meet you in the middle."

With sober regard, she nods at my command.

"You got it. Be careful, Omega."

"Always am. Same to you."

Without another word, we split. I wait until Chi rounds the corner, and I can hear her solid heels clicking up the stairs. It's still fairly dark, but my enhanced vision allows for a few additional details not afforded to your average human. It's not night vision, but it'll do just fine.

Good thing I brought my helm with me. Better to err on the side of caution. Once the solid metal and plastic have encased my delicate cranium, I pull up all forms of passive scanning with which this particular accessory is equipped. Capabilities include actual night vision, as well as thermal imaging. Vivid green light bathes my face as I make a straight path from the girls' sleeping area to the nearby southeast wall. The enhanced view draws everything into crisp, stark focus. There are telltale signs of rodents in the droppings scattered here and there. The tiny warm masses scurrying in and out of my vision are also readily apparent. But nothing human-size registers on the grid. No footprints in the dust or other signs that something more significant has passed through recently.

My audios are cranked to the highest I can take without the risk of blowing out my eardrums. The soft breaths escaping me magnify, sounding as if I'm loudly panting. There's a door set into the southern wall that initial scouting and assessment determined to be fused shut. Putting a gloved hand to its levered handle, I double-check with firm pressure and am met with solid resistance. No way that she went out through here.

Something shifts slightly, and my audios attune to the noise. Startled, I spin around only to be confronted with nothing. Cursing my unease, I wait patiently for whatever it is to make its presence known again. I don't have to wait long, only a handful of minutes, before the same sound echoes back. This time I pinpoint the direction, aided by the lack of sound elsewhere. There's no wind outside, and everyone's sleep is muted background noise. That's why this anomaly stands out so much.

My mind races as to what it could be as I wind my way through the tall columns of concrete and tile that support the upper floors of the building. The architect chose an open design for this office, leaving the supporting structure exposed with few walls to hide it.

Something about all of this gnaws at the back of my mind as being off. As I'm drawn closer to the next opening that reveals the upper levels, I know why. It's where I saw the girls meeting yesterday, having their secret soiree away from the others. And that's almost exactly where I locate our missing person.

That easily missed huffing sound comes from her as she tries and fails to push in a stairway door. We marked it as blocked and, therefore, secure, so we didn't bother to venture further. The faded yellow icon on the otherwise innocuous door promises stairs. It's basement access, with no staircase leading away above it. I'm stuck standing in dull surprise and confoundedness. What the hell is she doing? The young woman seems to be appraising the situation before she takes a few steps back and, with a running start, rams her shoulder against the sealed door with as much force as she can manage.

I puzzle over the intensity of her actions before something else registers. It's the same stink as before, now much more pronounced as she's managed to crack the door open by a couple of inches. It's putrid and vile, almost overwhelming the senses, and I'm still halfway across the room. Sadly, that's when things finally click for me in these wee hours, and I manage to put two and two together.

This is the origin of that odd smell I kept coming across, along with those faint sounds I dismissed as the local rat population. They were nails. Human fingernails. Loud and hungry moans echo out from the crack of black space.

"Shit!" I cry loudly, startling Kari as she stands in shock before the partially ajar fiberglass door.

Adrenaline floods my system in a heady rush so strong I taste blood on my tongue. I lunge forward, grabbing the girl's arm closest to me and flinging her behind and out of the way. My grip was probably too tight and left bruises. Add to that the impact from the strength behind my throw, but that can't be helped. I'm more concerned about the sudden mass of arms thrusting through the quickly widening slit in the doorway. The pale, damaged limbs claw against each other like thick, gray worms, raking each other, the wall, and the open space before them. Shaking the image out of my mind, I take the safety off my rifle while throwing the Comms channel wide.

"Broadcast all channels," I command the AI while slowly backing away from the newly exposed horde. "Code Zee. I repeat, Code Zee. We have an unknown number of Zee, floor level southeast corner. The blocked basement stairwell is exposed, and they're attempting to breach the door. I need all bodies with guns to my position. NOW!"

"Fuck!" I can't help the curse as I attempt to keep an eye on the threat and the civvie behind me.

"Kari!" I call as calmly as possible. The first head pokes through, and I immediately get it in the crosshairs and put a couple of rounds between its hazy eyes.

With no response, I glance her way. She's frozen in place, blank with shock. No doubt, the up close and personal view of gore and snarling creatures is a captivating sight.

"KARI!" I bark again. This time she manages to turn her attention to me briefly. Taking a chance, I hold her gaze for the few seconds it takes to impart my directions.

"Get your friends and head up to the northwest corner of the top floor. Stairs are right next to where you're all sleeping."

"Yeah…" she wavers.

"Northwest corner. Top floor. Got it?" My patience is just about gone, as is the bent hinge precariously keeping the enemy at bay.

"Yes. Got it." She seems to snap out of her daze and finally understands the enormity of what her prying has done.

"Then go. Now!"

I don't wait to hear her reply. Instead, my attention turns to the very loud and hungry Zee breaking out of their prison and acutely fixating on the nearest warm body. Oh, fuck, me.

Switching from semi to auto, I unload the first hailstorm of bullets aiming for where skulls and, therefore, brains should be. The ordnance we typically use is intended for maximum damage and penetration. I imagine the stairwell's wall is now riddled with holes, and many more are inevitably coming.

I hate spraying munitions everywhere like some damn hose. Such carelessness is how you go through your allotted ammo three months into a six-month mission. Any greenhorn worth their tainted salt knows it. Gritting my teeth, I mark how many Zee have stopped moving versus those still incoming behind them. I might have taken out 30% of the first batch if I'm lucky.

I can't help glowering at the overall crappy predicament our guests have managed to get us into. As the Zee advance, I attempt to put more of the open cubicle space between them and me. By my count, maybe two minutes have passed since I made the emergency call. I have another couple of minutes at most before my backup is here…hopefully.

I can't imagine a single one of my team is capable of sleeping through the kind of violence I'm producing.

Pop. Pop. Pop. Pop. Pop. Pop. Pop. Pop. Pop. Pop. Pop. Pop.

The subsequent influx of Zee starts pushing through their putdown kin. This time I take the extra few seconds I've bought myself to switch from auto to three-shot and actually aim at targets. I'll feel guilt over the waste of bullets later after I'm victorious and my hide is intact.

Strangely enough, it's the warped remains of hinges that finally decides to give in to the horde pushing so insistently at it and not the actual door. As that solid piece of faded redwood composite tumbles to the floor, I take another few steps away and prepare to run.

Not that I need to. Those snarling Zee are just getting to their misaligned feet when a shot whizzes by my right audio, nearly blowing out my eardrum with the resulting feedback. Wincing, I quickly raise a free hand and dial it down to a range that won't result in premature deafness.

Just as quickly, Rho is at my elbow, rifle raised and sighted, as he works on taking out the front line. To my left is, surprisingly, the Alpha, doing the same with the successive Zee. His helmet is in place, so all I can see of him is the bronzed gold of his Captain's helm.

THE SETTLING SUN

"**A**nd just what have you been up to, Omega?"

While teasing in Rho's voice brings levity to the situation, it is also super annoying. No sense downplaying a problem I may have prevented had I located the girl sooner.

"Fuck off, Rho, and try aiming, would you? If you can't shoot them, I'll just use your body as a barrier to prevent them from getting at me."

"Ooh, harsh, Megs. You wound me deeply."

"Not deeply enough," I mutter out of the side of my mouth.

"What's the situation, Commander?" Chi's cool voice cuts in. Very business-like, that one.

"Severely crapped up?" I reply with all of the sarcasm that I can muster. A grunt escapes me as I dodge the grimy swipe of some white-collared Zee. At least, I think it used to be white.

Climbing back into command mode, I reply a little less emotionally and a lot more authoritatively.

"Looks like the locals were barred down in the basement level. Probably been there a long while based on how worn they are, and feasting on the rats trapped with them and vice versa, I'd wager."

"Lovely."

"Yeah, definitely. Our illustrious missing guest had the bright idea of letting them out."

"So, what's the plan, boss?" Rho breaks in again.

"Our best bet is to reseal them, but we'll need to clear the door and weld it shut somehow."

"What I wouldn't give for a frag round," Chi laments.

"I know. Is there any chance you found something that can make a smallish boom?"

Chi's slender form pauses in its firing as she considers her options. We're low on munitions, and this debacle will set us back even more. Our next step has to be a restock depot, or we'll be pretty useless. And dead. Definitely not very alive.

"Ah!" she exclaims, voice pitched high in excitement. "Yes, I think that'll work. Can you give me twenty minutes, Commander?"

"Twenty?" I cry incredulously.

"Hey, that's pushing it. You want this done, right? I need that time."

"Ugh. Okay, fine." Like I have a choice. Turning, I address the sixth silent member of this firing squad.

"Tau. Back up Chi and help her get whatever she needs to make her explosives. While you're at it, keep an eye out for our guests. I told that fool, Kari, to relocate herself and the others to the top floor for safety. No guarantee that she heard me or did as she was told, but I'd rather not blow up some civvies along with the Zee if it can be helped. Even if they might have it coming." I finish darkly.

For a breath, he doesn't respond or stop shooting. I'm about to get mad before his line joins the group's Comms channel with a heavy sigh.

"Fine. What if they can't be detained?" is what he manages as a response. Better than usual, I guess.

"Do what you have to. Those women are a liability to us and a potential threat to the UF." Grim-faced he nods once in understanding.

Nodding back, I turn and all but shout to Chi, "Go!"

"See you in twenty," she smirks before slinging her rifle and leaving the room at a sprint. The Alpha follows close behind but has to work to match her speed. I allow myself a modicum of satisfaction before returning to the task. Twenty minutes. Okay. We can do this.

"You heard the lady, team. We need to keep them at bay for twenty. So do your best to conserve ammo. I don't need to tell you we're down to our last few cases."

"Crud," Rho comments. "Permission to engage in hand-to-hand?"

"Negative, Rho!" I bark impatiently before leveling my gun at a Zee's body. "I don't want anyone in that mess. We need to keep distance between them and us as long as we can."

He grunts in anger or exasperation before straightening up and re-engaging the enemy. It isn't the time for any argument. I'm in danger of having my hands and arms fatigue faster than usual with the death grip I'm keeping on my M4. I have difficulty easing up as I'm more concerned with the seemingly endless flow of Zee crawling out of the basement. How could there have been so many below? We were lax in having missed this risk.

The shape of the horde shifts imperceptibly, and I only have a moment to cry out, "Rho!" as a Zee breaks through their self-made line. Unlike its brethren, this one is not sloppy or slow. Its arms are held aloft, hands shaped into claws as it sprints hard and fast for my second. I get a glance of a fairly cleanly clothed Zee, not nearly as rotted as it should be. Almost like it's newly made. That shouldn't be right.

Rho may be on the lean side, but he is 6 feet, 6 inches tall and is solidly muscled. However, as this new Zee slams into his unprepared form, it simply lifts him off his feet like he's some lightweight.

That seems to put in motion some shift with the Zee as more sprinters stream out of the newly created gap. All are heading for my downed soldier with the utmost eagerness.

"Shit!" I cry out again. I stow my primary weapon and grab my baton, fully intending to bludgeon anything that gets in my way. A long leg garbed in UF fatigues kicks one offender away. With my arm pulled back, I take full swing at its head, caving it in.

Flecks of gore fly up as I pull my baton back, ready for the next. It's none too soon as another one leaps over Rho's downed form. Its hands are stretched towards me, eager to catch whatever it can. I grab one of its frail wrists and pull the Zee and its rank odor past me. Once it's in an unoccupied space, the team drills it into the ground.

I handle the next few that come at me similarly, forcing them past me to the others waiting for them. There's no point in wasting time and energy on these one-offs. My goal lies before me, quite literally. Wading through the group of mismatched bodies, I pull dead and undead creatures off my hopefully still-alive gunner. Sweat runs down my neck and spine, sliding beneath the armored suit encasing me from neck to ankle. A Zee finally notices me in the thick of things and changes its focus. Jaws clamp hard onto my gauntlet-clad forearm, unforgiving.

I can't help the grunt that escapes me as my limb is squeezed within its metal surroundings by a ceaseless vise. It renders my right arm temporarily useless, but thankfully I'm possessed of a second, still free arm, and I bring that unyielding, ironwood rod down again and again against its unprotected neck. Something gives way with a crunch of finality, and the inflexible grip is released.

Pushing the corpse aside, I frantically call to my second.

"Rho! Can you hear me?"

Silence is the only answer I receive both over the Comms and externally. I feel my blood pressure rise. Fear and anxiety catch my breath, and for a moment, I'm propelled to a different time and place in my mind. This can't be happening. Not again.

"Fuck! Omega?" The gunner's cry reaches me through the pile of churning, writhing bodies and catalyzes me into action.

"I'm coming. Hang on!"

I dive headfirst into the mess, grabbing onto whatever flesh or cloth is within reach and wrenching it away from my fallen brother. The joint of whatever I'm handling dislocates as it pulls at the attached Zee awkwardly. With its limb pulled out of the socket, I reverse its momentum at the last moment, back toward me. My bar clubs it solidly along the upper half of its head, removing mangy grayed hair and fragments of bone.

"Omicron?" I call over my shoulder. I don't know where exactly he is in the fray. I can't see anybody from my position, but I know my Comms are working just fine. "Help me un-bury Rho."

"On it!" I hear him call through my headset. I'm quickly joined by a body almost twice my size.

"Head down," the medic grunts as he gives a yell of exertion, throwing his strength into heaving the flat side of his weapon through the throng of Zee. Those unfortunate enough to be standing taller than their brethren bear the brunt of its impact. The massive force behind his swing plows the Zee into a nearby yellowed stucco wall. The impact shatters both the monster and the column. Omicron's backswing delivers the same punishment to another group. Reminds me of some morbid pendulum.

With half an eye towards when and where he's swinging, I duck and look for the opportunity to lunge after one of those taupe-colored lanky legs still kicking and pushing beneath the writhing mass. With the slightest hint of a grip on him, I roughly haul at Rho's form, doing my best not to accidentally separate his leg from his torso. In the heat of battle, controlling my strength is more complicated than it sounds.

My pulling manages to get him clear of the dogpile while inadvertently toppling the remaining handful of gray-skinned Zee onto each other. That's fine, though. Om takes advantage of the mess by bringing the solid weight of his god hammer down again and again.

I do my best to ignore the sick, squelching, cracking sounds coming from my medic's way. Definitely NOT "Do no harm." That random, morbid thought strangely amuses me.

I pull Rho up against a nearby wall as we both need to catch our breath, and I need to know what the damage is. Half-consciously I catalog and compartmentalize that Mu is still firing rhythmically behind us. There's not much time to hug and take care of Rho's ouchies, though. Instead, I start liberally patting the guy down. The gunner pulls his helm free with a gasp as I do so.

"Shit!" he exclaims when I press against his right side.

For a moment, our eyes meet—mine through the visored glass. He's shaken. That's to be expected. I can feel the accelerated staccato of his heartbeat through where my hand is still in contact with his rib cage. For the type of work we do, it's rare for us to be vulnerable to the enemy. Most of the how and what of our job is a tried and true process.

Rho quirks a sardonic smile that's overshadowed by his pain.

"Sorry, boss. Didn't expect that to happen."

His smile turns to a grimace as I further prod the new wound. Flipping the top of my faceplate, I get a better look at the spot. No visible seepage from blood or tears in the clothing and, therefore, skin. It's between the edge of his flak vest and the top of his belt. The Zee couldn't have planned it better if it had been intentional.

"Idiot. It would help if you watched your three better. Just because you have an extra level of protection there doesn't mean you get lazy."

Despite the content of my words, my tone is decidedly softer than I'd desired.

"Yeah, I know. One of 'em landed on me just right, or maybe just wrong. Feels like something's not right here." He gestures down to the tender region of his side.

Biting my cheek, I press the spot with a little more restraint. There's an odd give to it, but there's no way that I can tell if he's acquired some internal damage or not. We'll need Omicron's high-res scanners for that. There's also no scent of blood in the air other than the putrid odor of whatever you call the stuff that oozes out of Zee.

"Okay. That settles it."

Easily, yet somewhat awkwardly, I heft his taller form up, slinging an arm over my shoulder while carefully supporting the opposite side. Together we make our way back behind our remaining teammates. They're both on rifles now and positioned such that they're side by side. There's no doubt that they're trying to conserve ammo. I try to calculate how long it's been since Chi and Tau ran off. Can twenty minutes have possibly passed? I seem to have lost track of time between taking on our new Zee friends and rescuing Rho's bony ass. Worrying my lip, I check my ammo clip and am dismayed at what remains. This is not good.

"Mu. Om. How are you holding up?"

"Barely, Omega," Omicron huffs. "Got another four magazines, then I'm toast."

"Fine," is all I get from the young sniper. Well, that's worrisome.

"Mu?" I press again, concerned.

She hesitates, and that's even more telling.

"Last mag, Omega."

Crud.

"I've still got a few left," my downed teammate offers through clenched teeth.

Glancing back his way, I can see a line of sweat along the bone of his high brow. His eyes are clear and focused, though, so that's a good sign. Nodding once, I hold out a dirty, gloved hand.

"Great. Gimme."

Shifting a little to the side, he produces a set of three magazines and dutifully hands them over. I make sure he still has some ammo left for himself, along with his sidearm, before I return to the meat of the battle.

Coming alongside the blue-haired sniper, I warn her of my approach before tapping the back of her shoulder. I do a quick handoff of ammo for her M4. She immediately slams home the first magazine into the space beneath her weapon. The other two are stowed swiftly into empty pockets in her vest. As one, we all refocus on the growing crowd of Zee that seem to keep coming. How many could there possibly be below? There's something wrong with this setup. The room is filled with the sounds of flesh and clothing rubbing sinuously against one another as the Zee gnash their decaying teeth and moan lustily in their eagerness to get at us.

Pointing the business end directly at the face of what looks like some road worker, iridescent vest, and all, it seems there are more bodies here than can be attributed to the 8 to 5 business types you'd expect. My finger flicks a centimeter, and his face explodes, a few drops splattering against my face shield. Doesn't matter. These bastards have to go. We're surviving this.

I'm getting dangerously low on ammo, so I make the split-second decision to swap my primary weapon for sidearms. With the safety flicked off, I take two steps forward, feeling lighter with my handguns than I ever do carting around an M4. Choosing my targets, I unload. Mu's clean shots join mine, piercing the space right over my shoulder, but I trust my sniper and her sure-shot ways.

She takes the back, I've got the front, and Om's clearing the sides. It's satisfying just putting these Zee down so succinctly.

"Incoming behind, you guys." Chi's clear voice breaks through the carnage we're immersed in.

I pause to glance over my shoulder and catch sight of her nearly flying down the hall in her haste. Tau follows closely in her wake, a silent shadow. They level with our line, and I redirect my attention to the following two targets. Without pause, I address my demo lady.

"Chi. What took you so long?"

"Oh, you know. I needed my all-natural, eco-conservative coffee. I couldn't find anything organic, so I went with the day's flavor."

She holds up a broad tin can in my peripheral sight. Trying to look at it while being unable to entirely, I'm confused for a second and can't help but dumbly comment.

"It's a coffee can."

"Oh, most certainly," she responds jovially. Directing her attention towards the enemy with narrowed eyes, she continues, "It's also our salvation."

"Say what?"

"I need a path to their center to plant it, and then we need to haul ass out of here."

"Like, how out of here are we talking?" Eyeing our surroundings, I try to recall what is still spread out in our makeshift camp and not ready for our impending bug-out.

Seeming to read my thoughts, she replies quietly. "I gave us a few minutes to clear the structure and an extra 40 feet of ground for good measure."

"That's not all that generous," I respond dubiously.

"Precisely."

She seems rather pleased with herself. That's a scary thought. Shit. Okay, no choice. Thinking quickly, I pull up the group Comms and cue the rest of the team to our plan.

"Alright, guys, we have an idea. Tau, you and I need to create a thirty-second hole near the basement entrance for Chi to leave her gift. In the meantime, Omicron, I need you to cart Rho's butt to his bike. Mu, you follow and cover their retreat. Grab whatever necessities you can from camp and clear out. You all have T-minus 90 seconds after you leave the space to be clear of the building."

There's a quick chorus of affirmations, including Chi indicating her readiness. Omicron hustles over to where Rho is slumped down and lifts him in one go. Slinging the gunner's left arm over his broad shoulders, he makes ready to book—gangly cargo in tow. That's all the preparation needed for me to greenlight things.

"Okay, Chi. Do it."

"Roger." And she's off.

While her lithe figure cuts through the enemy, my rounds take out everything moving on the other end. I mark Tau's rifle lying down a similar path along the right. Long legs extend as Chi pushes herself forward, awkward cargo clutched to her chest plate. She athletically leaps over the first few fallen Zee, nimbly dodging around another two like an experienced football quarterback before sliding along in a side tackle that would make any soccer player proud. Rubber soles plant and brace as a high-pitched screech heralds her skidding to a halt directly in front of the unhinged doorway.

She must be hard-pressed for breath after that and even more so with the horde clamoring down on her. However, that soldier is calm under pressure, making her perfect for handling ordinance when steady hands and a clear mind are an absolute requirement. Even then... glancing at the hand clutching her homemade explosive, I ruefully recall the missing digits on her left. Chi may be a perfectionist by nature, but she still makes mistakes. It's a good thing to keep in mind that we're all fallible. We have to bank on her making those mistakes as few and far between as possible, especially right now.

I'm holding my breath as she places the coffee-can-turned-IED at the entrance. Shiny gray duct tape appears out of nowhere and is quickly wound around both cylinder and frame, securing it in place. A flick of her fingers and a flash occurs, creating a spark that greedily latches on to the makeshift fuse.

Chi has the best gadgets out of all of us, and her flint-tipped gloves are no exception.

Once she's confident the fire catches hold, the demolitionist straightens up, bugging out of there. I take care of the first Zee waiting for her with a hole through its skull. Chi doesn't flinch as gore splatters at her face and lands in her violet locks. The Zee that dodges from the side, trying to get in a quick bite as she runs by, loses its lower jaw to Tau's marksmanship. And so it proceeds as she approaches, and we backpedal. Us clearing the way and her trying to get clear. I wait until I feel the barest tap on my left shoulder as she splits the ground between the Alpha and me before pulling up and following closely after her.

I don't have to visually check to know that Tau is following my lead, as sensors confirm this indirectly for me. The three of us put our all into reaching the bikes parked along the far side of the building. The seconds tick down mentally with each hurried step. I'm glad this takes place on the ground floor, so we're not contending with stairs or the like.

Our exit brings us through the center of the complex and where the interlopers slept. I notice that their belongings are nowhere to be found. Frickin' ungrateful bastards. I don't blame them for prioritizing their survival, however, they caused this mess. I'm convinced there was no accident in their doing so, either.

"Cowards," Tau spits, cutting through Comms. I'm surprised by the suddenness of it, as well as by my alignment with his thought processes. I don't have the luxury of time to dwell on it, and worrying for my other teammates takes priority.

"Omega, this is Rho," my second's voice cuts in quickly. It sounds like he's speaking through gritted teeth. "We're clear. On bikes heading to a safe evac point, hopefully. Coordinates are transmitting to your bikes now."

Just as he finishes his broadcast, we clear the outer door and see our three gorgeous behemoths ready and waiting.

Grinning ferally, I respond, "Roger that, Rho. Just mounting up now. We'll see you in a few, barring being blown up."

Not bothering with decorum or propriety, I hop onto my bike like I'm straddling a horse from the Wild West. All hard thunks, I flick on the throttle, Comms line, and GPS, one right after the other. The ATC is rumbling in sync with its brethren as I release its lock and lurch backward, nearly being thrown from my beast by the sudden acceleration.

I glance at my mirrors and see the other two under my command are close behind. Even closer behind them, bodies begin to pour out of our former B&B's entrance in a frenzy to get at us.

"That was close," Chi remarks glibly, voice light in my audios.

Weirdly positive tone aside, I have to agree. That said, we have all of ten seconds before things go kaboom.

"Chi…" I begin.

"I know, Omega. Almost clear. Just a little further."

My countdown is at five seconds now.

"How much more?" I grind out, focusing on the rapidly shrinking building in my rearview.

"Um…brace yourselves?" Is all that she offers.

"Fuh…" is all I get out before the office and surrounding structure are engulfed in a pillar of fire. A shockwave quickly follows in its wake.

I clench my thighs firmly against the padded metal of my cycle before hell rains down. Closed, sweaty palms encased in leather hold a death grip on the handles of the ATC. I feel my rear tire lift from the ground. Chunks of concrete land like large hailstones along our path. Couple that with the myriad of tiny bits of shrapnel falling and pinging us and our bikes, and it's like a storm of metal and rock. There's a sick clench to my stomach as I anticipate being thrown or flipped, and then there's that brief moment of vertigo that's just as quickly relinquished. Thankfully, just as the explosion's heat crossed our backsides, it started receding. The roar of three strong motors gains strength in my audios.

Holy crap. We only just cleared it. Not quite sure how I feel about that close call.

To be sure, I glance through my side mirrors and mark the locations of my cohorts relative to myself as they begin to ease on their throttles and drift. It is by no means our most narrow escape but still uncomfortably close. Having a fireball trying to toast your assets is no fun.

I loosen my death grip on the throttle as we near the first half of the team. All three are stopped and seated on their ATCs at the coordinates Rho supplied. The space is empty of anyone else and anything remotely alive as we slow to a halt before them. My second is leaning forward slightly to the right, cradling his rib cage with his left hand as the alloy-coated metal of his right arm supports most of his weight.

Sometimes it's difficult to tell which arm of his is flesh and bone and which one's not when he's all suited up properly from head to toe.

Now, though, his right hand is gloveless and exposed. I don't miss the slight intake of breath over my left shoulder. I surmise our resident Alpha must have missed that detail about the gunner before now. If it wouldn't bring so much focus on Rho, I'd needle Tau over his inattention. Hmm…maybe a saver for later?

What brought about Rho's prosthetic arm isn't entirely known to me. I'm curious as fuck, sure. Who wouldn't be? The little I've gotten him to share over the years resulted from consuming an elderly bottle of bourbon during some rare downtime. Even then, the details provided were rather slim. I am privy to the fact that it's UF-made and was installed after his genetic upgrade. It's also directly connected to the warped Christian cross he always wears. Something about a church and a fire during pre-Zeta soldier days.

What that does mean is he's permanently indebted to the United Forces. That kind of tech does not come cheap. Add to that regular upkeep and maintenance, and I'm reasonably sure that's a hefty bill he will have to pay in some form or another. One more glance at the dark metal of his manufactured knuckles, and I let the questions in my mind fall away—this time. Looking up, I'm met with the gunner's carmine eyes. I'd wager that he did not miss my earlier assessment or the Alpha's slip-up. Moving on.

"Report."

Clearing his throat, the tall soldier does his best to straighten on his bike and shrug off any obvious discomfort.

"We managed to pack up most of the camp, but some clothing and extra foodstuffs were left behind. Overall, we got clear with the remainder of our munitions, med gear, and some standard food rations."

Sighing, I lean back in my seat a little. "That's a relief. I take it no sign of our guests?"

Shaking his head, he confirms. "Nope. They were long gone before we passed their sleeping quarters. I'm guessing they hauled ass as soon as shit went down."

"Lovely." My lip curls in disgust. "They throw the party, and we're left to clean up and sort out their mess." It wasn't a coincidence that they were in this area. What that damned woman did seemed calculated. But to what end? What the hell was she hoping to find in there?

"Yeah." He blows the next syllable through pursed lips. "So, are we going after them?"

Glancing towards the rising sun along the horizon, I give the idea solid thought. There was something amiss with their whole setup. They were too eager to make camp with us. Too accepting of being around Zeta soldiers. It's been a while since we interacted directly with civilians, and I'd overlooked the lack of distrust and utter hatred our presence typically tends to garner. They could be tied into that Light of Life group or whatever they're called. Those zealots have questionable motives regarding the future of humanity, but that's way above my meager pay grade. It's my fault for going against basic instincts and extending some modicum of trust to outsiders. Won't happen again.

Unsurprisingly, our overall supplies are dangerously scant, and I would like to rectify this.

"No." I hold a hand up, forestalling any argument. "We need to get to a depot before our next mission. Chasing down suspicious civvies isn't an option on our to-do list."

With a deep breath, I release the mounting tension and focus on the present and our near future.

"Mu, I want you to ensure you record the specifics of what occurred in our files. Send it in the next packet to HQ and mark it as a high priority for review. Let's leave it to the powers that be to make the call. If they want any answers, they can figure out the logistics." She nods in affirmation, all levity about her gone for the moment. I'm sure it'll return shortly.

Stretching, I throw a sardonic grin at my sniper. "Frankly, I don't feel like making any more out-of-the-box decisions today."

Just like that, she grins back, equally happy. Tau snorts inelegantly behind me, though I'm sure it's not out of humor. As I assess his aloof demeanor, I throw a narrow-eyed glare. He's far too much like the high-achieving jocks I dealt with in high school. All self-admiration and posturing. I do the best thing I can and turn around, dismissing the Alpha and refocusing on Rho and now Omicron.

The broader of the two opted to leave the seat of his bike in the interest of sorting out the gunner's injuries. He's got his portable med scanner out and is running what I think of as a mini MRI over Rho's side. He pushes the thinner man's hands out of the way as they keep flitting back protectively. Planting his own gloved fingertips dead center on Rho's chest, Om pins him in place like a bug.

Sitting patiently in the saddle, I await his assessment, leaning comfortably back. There's another hiss from the lankier of the two before Om leans away to review the scanner.

"Hmm," he murmurs as a thick thumb rubs his chin.

"Hmm, what?" I prompt.

Shaking his head, he folds the solidly enforced device closed with a resounding click. Eyebrow raised, he gives me the look of someone with infinitely more patience than I can ever hope to achieve in this life.

"Looks like he cracked one of his false ribs and bruised the other two above it. Thankfully, no full breaks and no internal bleeding. The flesh around the area already shows the bruising, but nothing too serious."

Addressing his patient directly, he continues, "Not much I can do about it. You need to take it as easy as possible and breathe deeply.

It will hurt for a few weeks, but you'll be back to normal in a month or so. Just don't go reinjuring that area and turning it into an actual break." Putting on his best stone face, Omicron finishes, "Then, I'll have to make it truly suck for you."

Sagging down into his seat, Rho is swathed in abject misery. A high-pitched whine leaves him mostly inadvertently. "No fair."

Now I'm the one who can't help but snort.

"Consider it your karma for dallying with those girls. Maybe next time, try thinking with your upper brain."

There are snickers all around at that, and the mood lifts slightly. Smiling thinly, I call over to Chi. She shifts her faceplate away once she's closer to my position.

"Chi, I need you to plot our course to the nearest refill station." Turning to the rest of the group, I include them in the next set of orders. "I'll give everyone five minutes to compose yourselves, and then we're heading out. Let's get back to full capacity within the next seventy-two hours. Got it?"

"You got it, boss," the spy responds wryly for all, head down as she pulls up her bike's GPS and compares that to known resupply stations.

There are plenty of UF supply stations to be found if you know where to look. These unmanned bunkers are far more efficient than having actual, fully manned outposts with all the drama and maintenance that goes along with them. Mind you, they're not precisely noted on any standard map or scan and are relatively innocuous if you don't know what you're looking for. All the better for us to avoid giving unauthorized individuals some free gear.

At the minimum, I'll be glad to have Chi fully outfitted with her professional-grade explosives again. Coffee cans are a bit too unstable for my taste.

Not too much later, our destination is set, and we're back on the move. I'm glad to bid goodbye to this area; there have been too many strange occurrences in one sitting for my taste.

Speak of the peculiar, had we lingered another fifteen minutes or so and happened to glance westward, we would have encountered a most unexpected sight; a very familiar wagon train meeting a larger group of people on foot similar in garb and locomotion. Forty to fifty travelers carrying a brilliant banner of white, the flag billowing in the warm breeze. Emblazoned upon its side is a yellow sun ringed in red, like a naked eye burning brightly for all who behold it.

FIN

ACKNOWLEDGMENTS

This story and this book have been a labor of soul and mind. I want to thank my family, first and foremost for all of their support, guidance, and patience. Without you the shiny things would have won out. Thank you to all of my friends and colleagues who kindly provided their unique perspectives and honest feedback when I thrust this story upon them.

A separate thank you to all of the service men and women, and their families and supporters. You are the ones who labor to protect our freedom and safety, at the risk of your own.

ABOUT THE AUTHOR

O. T. Riesen started life as an Army brat, beginning on the East Coast of the United States and finishing on the West with her parents and younger sister. A Jill of all trades, she's an avid reader, writer, and artist who enjoys expressing her overactive imagination in whatever form it takes. She currently calls Northern California home and resides there with her beloved family.

For more information about current and future works and endeavors by this author, visit marapublishing.com.

Made in the USA
Monee, IL
07 March 2023

29085243R00144